THE BOY, THE BIRD & THE COFFIN MAKER

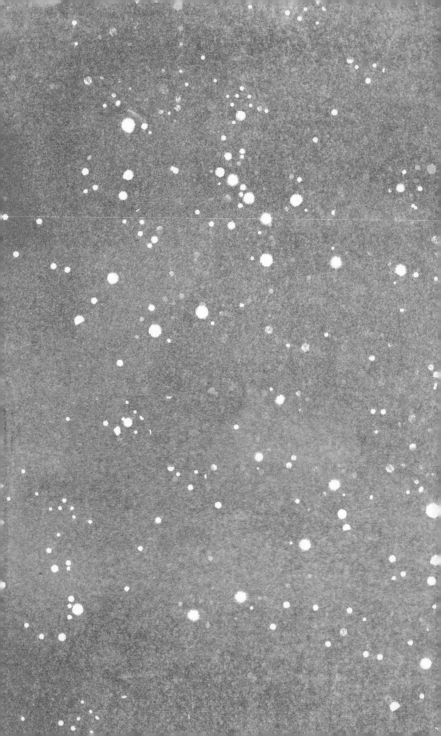

THE BOY, THE BIRD & THE COFFIN MAKER

Matilda Woods

Illustrated by Anuska Allepuz

Philomel Books

PHILOMEL BOOKS
an imprint of Penguin Random House LLC
375 Hudson Street, New York, NY 10014

Text copyright © 2017, 2018 by Matilda Woods.
Illustrations copyright © 2017 by Anuska Allepuz.
First American edition published by Philomel Books in 2018.
Published in Great Britain by Scholastic Ltd in 2017.

Philomel Books is a registered trademark of
Penguin Random House LLC.
Library of Congress Cataloging-in-Publication Data
Names: Woods, Matilda, author. | Allepuz, Anuska, 1979– author.
Title: The boy, the bird, and the coffin maker / Matilda Woods ;
illustrated by Anuska Allepuz. | Description: First American edition. |
New York, NY : Philomel Books, 2018. | Summary: Alberto, the town's
coffin maker, and Tito, a runaway boy, both lonely after suffering
tragic losses, learn the power of friendship as they try to escape the
shadows of their pasts. | Identifiers: LCCN 2017041775 |
ISBN 9780525515210 (hardback) | ISBN 9780525515227 (ebook)
| Subjects: | CYAC: Carpenters—Fiction. | Runaways—Fiction. |
Loneliness—Fiction. | Loss (Psychology)—Fiction. | Friendship—
Fiction. | BISAC: JUVENILE FICTION / Fantasy & Magic. | JUVENILE
FICTION / Family / Orphans & Foster Homes. | JUVENILE
FICTION / Social Issues / Death & Dying. |
Classification: LCC PZ7.1.W663 Bo 2018 | DDC [Fic]—dc23
LC record available at https://lccn.loc.gov/2017041775
Printed in the United States of America.
ISBN 9780525515210
1 3 5 7 9 10 8 6 4 2

American edition edited by Brian Geffen.
American edition designed by Jennifer Chung.
Text set in ITC Berkeley Oldstyle Std.

To my family—
those with two legs and four

THE COFFIN MAKER'S
FIRST COFFIN

The town of Allora was famous for two things. The first was its flying fish, and the second was the beauty of its winding streets. Tourists came from all over the country to watch the fish fly out of the sea while artists came to paint, in pigment, the bright houses that rose like steps up Allora Hill. There were so many colors that the artists did not have enough pigments to paint them, and it was rumored (at least by the Finestra sisters) that the great artist Giuseppe Vernice had invented a whole new color just to paint the roof of their house.

"Splendid Yolk, it was called," Rosa Finestra said to anyone who would listen.

"Derived from the crushed eye of a peacock feather," Clara Finestra added with a wise nod.

Yet though the sisters gushed about their bright home, the one next door was even brighter.

Alberto Cavello's house was the highest house on the hill. If you went any higher, you would reach the graveyard at the top. It stood like a bright azure jewel glistening across the sea. And it wasn't just bright. It was loud. It was loud when Alberto and his wife, Violetta, moved in. It grew louder when their first child, a girl named Anna Marie, was born; louder still when their son, Antonio, came into the world; and even louder when a little miracle named Aida wailed for the first time within its bright walls.

Alberto was a carpenter, the best in all of Allora. During the day he would build beds, tables and chairs for his paying clients, and at night he would build toys for his children.

With each new toy Alberto made, a new sound filled the house: squeals of delight as Anna Marie jumped off her spinning chair, screams of anger as Aida cried for Antonio to give back her favorite doll, and cries of "Gallop on! Gallop on!" as this same Antonio raced his wooden horse up and down the stairs.

Their house remained bright, loud and bustling for seven happy years until the sickness came.

The sickness appeared in the coldest month of winter, but it did not reach Allora until spring.

The first to fall ill were the men working on a new railway that linked Allora to the north, then the doctors who tended them and the artists who had come to paint the town. Only one family was wealthy enough to flee. The mayor took himself and his family on a long holiday to a place the sickness had not reached.

"Good luck!" he cried over his fat shoulder as a plush coach drawn by six white stallions carried them far away.

In the beginning, the dead were buried in the graveyard—one, then two, then three to a single plot—but as the sickness spread, other measures had to be taken.

A gate was built at the back of the graveyard and a thin staircase carved into the stone with steps leading down to the water. No longer buried, the dead were wrapped in blankets and cast out into the violent, surging sea.

As the number of dead mounted and the number of living fell, the cobbled streets of Allora grew quiet. Houses went unpainted, and shutters, once thrown open to greet spring, were pulled tightly closed. Even the Finestra sisters didn't poke their big noses out.

Just like the unfinished paintings that lay abandoned in the streets, the town of Allora itself began to fade.

The sickness rose up the hill—house by house— until it finally reached Alberto's home.

It took the eldest child first. Alberto spotted the purple mark behind Anna Marie's left ear as she read a book in her favorite chair. Then Antonio fell ill. While he was ailing in his bed, the mark came upon little Aida.

Violetta and Alberto tended to each child as they fell sick. They kissed them when they cried, hugged them when they whimpered, and when the time came for each of them to leave this world behind, they answered, "Yes, of course: one day, we will meet again."

Keeping her promise, Violetta joined them two days later. The plague bearers came to collect their bodies that evening, but Alberto wouldn't let them.

"I can't," he had said to the two men waiting at the front door. "I can't let you throw them away. Not into that cruel sea." Even from where he stood outside the highest house on Allora Hill, Alberto could see foam shooting up from where the waves crashed against the gray stones below. He could not bear to think of his family thrown in there.

"You must get rid of them somehow," the men had replied. "You can't let them stay inside. It will spread the sickness quicker."

"I'll bury them."

"All the coffin makers are dead. We collected the last one this morning."

"Then I'll make their coffins myself."

And that is what Alberto did. He went into his workshop and for the first time built something for the dead instead of the living. He carved a coffin for his wife, a coffin for his eldest daughter, a coffin for his only son, and a coffin for little Aida. Each was smaller than the one before and, like babushka dolls, could fit inside the other.

When the coffins were finished and his family buried, Alberto returned to his workshop and began to make his own. But by the time he finished, the plague had left the town. The mayor returned from his holiday, the Finestra sisters reopened their shutters, and people passed gaily up and down the streets of Allora once more.

But instead of joining them, Alberto sat beside his coffin every day, alone, waiting for the purple mark to come back and claim him too.

THE BOY AND THE BIRD

Thirty Years Later

The boy stared out the window of the train. Steam billowed out of the chimneys and drifted up into the mountains. The boy had never seen mountains so tall or so wild. They reached above the clouds and stretched farther than his eyes could see.

"You'll be flying out there in no time," the boy whispered to a small bird peering out of his pocket. She was enjoying the view too. "As soon as your wing is better, you'll be able to fly to the top of the tallest mountain in the world."

"Twrp," the bird said with a small nod of her head. When the boy first found her, two months before, she had been black all over. But now sometimes, when the sun shone on her wings or when she ate a particularly tasty treat, her feathers would flash gold or silver or green in the light. Today, they were flashing all three. She must have been very happy.

"You must know where we're going," the boy whispered to his bird. "Everyone who goes to Allora is happy. That's what my mum says. She says that Allora is the brightest and happiest place in the whole world."

When she heard the word *Allora*, the bird's feathers grew even brighter, and she let out a loud trill that made several passengers on the train jump.

"That's right," the boy said with a bright laugh. "Allora is going to be amazing. Mum says that in Allora you never get hungry because the fish jump out of the sea and straight into your mouth. She says you never get cold because even in winter the sun keeps the snow away. And, best of all, Mum says that Allora is so far away from everything else that once we get there, he'll never find us again."

When she heard the final sentence, the bird's

wings darkened and she pulled her head back into the boy's pocket.

"Don't worry," the boy said to his little best friend. "Mum promised we'll be safe this time."

But despite the boy's assurances, the bird refused to look out of his pocket, and for the rest of the train journey south, her feathers remained a deep shade of black. While the boy was convinced of Allora's safety, the bird, it appeared, was not.

THE MAYOR'S EARLY ORDER

One Year Later

I want it made of golden oak," said the mayor grandly. "Nothing beats golden oak. Strong as an ox and light as a feather. They say—" He tried to lean across the table, but his vast stomach got in the way. "You can throw a whole tree in the ocean, roots and all, and it would float all the way to the shores of Africa."

"Are you planning a sea burial?" Alberto asked. He wasn't used to asking questions. His clients were usually dead by the time they arrived.

"Of course not," the mayor spat. "I'm not a sailor."

"No one in Allora is," Alberto agreed. No man, sane or insane, would set sail across that tumultuous sea.

Almost as if it had heard, the sea chose this moment to send a colossal wave crashing into the rocks below. Water sprayed so high it battered the kitchen window. A second later, a giant sea bass battered it too. Luckily, it didn't break the glass.

"So," Alberto said as the fish flapped about on the cobbles outside, "why do you want it to float?"

"I don't." The mayor took a sip of his tea and then, tasting it, spat it back out. He only drank tea steeped from the finest leaves, and Alberto's were clearly the cheapest.

"But you just sai—"

"Oh, I don't care about all that floating nonsense." The mayor flapped his hand about like the fish in the lane outside. "I just care that it's . . ." He searched for the right word. "Rare!"

"And expensive," Alberto added. You couldn't buy a more expensive wood, not unless you shipped it in from Africa itself. "Are you sure you don't want to use something else, like elder wood or ash?"

The mayor gave him a scathing look. "I'm not poor, Coffin Maker."

Alberto eyed the mayor's golden lace and velvet cloak. "No one could ever accuse you of being that. Golden oak it is." He dipped his pen into a jar of ink and wrote *Golden Oak* beneath the mayor's name. "Now." He looked up from his notebook. "Measurements."

"Measurements?" The mayor lost some of his vigor. "What measurements?"

"*Your* measurements, Mr. Mayor. Height and girth will do. After all, I'm no shoemaker."

In truth, there were no shoemakers in Allora. Not anymore. The last one had died two weeks before. Alberto had made his coffin:

Master Luigi Scarpa
Elder wood
75 × 23 inches

"Er, right. Well . . ."

"I have a tape measure," Alberto offered. "I could get it if you would like."

"No. No. It's quite all right." The mayor waved him back into his seat. "We can leave the measurements for now."

16

"I'm afraid I can't do much without measurements. They're a vital part of the coffin-making process. Normally, I'd measure the body myself. Most people don't come to me when they're still alive."

"Well, I'm not like most people, am I? I'm the mayor, the mayor of all Allora." He stuck his chest out importantly, and the fat of his stomach broke over the edge of the table. "And as the mayor it's my right, nay, my responsibility, to have the largest and grandest coffin this town has ever seen."

He'll certainly have the largest, Alberto thought to himself. He had never met anyone, alive or dead, who was as fat as the mayor.

"What was that?" the mayor snapped.

Alberto's eyes widened. Had he said that out loud?

"On second thought, I think it was my stomach." The mayor hauled it back under the table. "She always gets temperamental in the evenings. You don't happen to have any cakes or sweets in the cupboard? Just to quell the gentle beast." He gave his stomach a fond rub and glanced hopefully around the kitchen.

"There's some stale bread on the bench," Alberto offered. "And some cheese on that plate. It's looking a bit green, but it might taste okay."

"Never mind," the mayor said, though he looked like he minded a lot.

"So?" Alberto asked.

"So, what?"

"What are your measurements? Just an estimate will do, so I can order the wood. If you want the grandest coffin, I'll have to start work on it soon."

"Right, well, seventy inches by—er ..." The mayor's fat cheeks turned a deep shade of red. "Seventy inches, I suppose."

"Seventy by seventy?" Alberto said, unable to hide his surprise.

"What's wrong with that?"

"There's nothing wrong with it. It's just curious."

"What's curious?"

"I usually make rectangular coffins, not square ones."

"If it's too much of a challenge," the mayor said, trying unsuccessfully to stand up, "I'm sure I can find someone else to build it."

"It's no problem at all, Mr. Mayor." Alberto dipped his pen into the ink and wrote the measurements down. "Now ..." His voice wavered. He had a feeling the mayor would not appreciate the next question. "When would you like it by?"

The mayor's face turned from red to purple. "How would I know?" he blustered. "One doesn't exactly *know* these things. Death can be very unexpected."

"It always is," the coffin maker agreed. "One moment you're breathing, and the next you're not."

"Still," the mayor said with a nervous laugh, "you shouldn't work too fast. I'm not planning on popping off anytime soon."

Outside, the clock tower rising from the graveyard chimed twelve. To block the tolls, the mayor began to yell.

"Good genes, I have. Mother lived to eighty-three, and even then she was killed by a runaway cart. Clean bill of health except for the broken skull and punctured lu—"

The mayor was cut off by three loud knocks on the front door. He frowned and looked across the table to Alberto.

"Do you usually have visitors this late?"

"Not living ones," the coffin maker said, and leaving the mayor alone in the kitchen, he went to answer the door.

"Put her down there." Alberto pointed to a table near the back of his workshop. He had carried a

candle from the kitchen and now used it to light five more around the room. One by one, little pools of yellow-gray light spluttered into life. When they formed one constant glow, he joined the two men who had carried the body in.

Alberto recognized the woman. It was Miss Bonito. She had moved to Allora just over a year ago. In the four seasons she had called the town home, Alberto had spoken to her only once. He had helped her to read a sign in the market square: Two pears for the price of one!

"What happened?" Alberto asked. He knew both men, one far better than the other. The older man was Enzo the baker, and the younger was his apprentice, Santos.

"She died," Santos said.

"I can see that. How did she die?"

"Um . . ." Santos looked to his master.

"A growth, Alberto." Enzo coughed to clear his throat. "Right there. Just above her heart." He pointed toward her chest, where, above the cut of her faded dress, a lump the size of a small apple could be seen.

"Ah," Alberto said sadly. "I have seen this type of thing before. Many a time, in fact." He pulled back from the body and looked at his old friend Enzo. "Who found her?"

"My wife. She used to give her our stale loaves for free. Poor thing couldn't afford them fresh. Hadn't seen her for two weeks, so my wife went out to the cottage to check if she was okay. Found her like this, alone in her bed, the sheets still warm."

"Warm?" Alberto frowned. "Are you sure?" By the state and smell of her, he was certain Miss Bonito had been dead for at least a week. If it had been high summer, she would not have even looked like Miss Bonito anymore.

"Si. Si, Alberto," Enzo said with a sad nod and even sadder eyes. "My wife was most sure about that."

Ah, Alberto thought. That explained it. Enzo's wife was prone to exaggeration, almost as much as the Finestra sisters, who lived next door.

"She could not afford food, Alberto, let alone a coffin." Enzo's voice took on the tone of a proud man about to ask a favor. "But I remember—how could I forget?—that you helped my father when we couldn't afford . . ."

"Of course. Of course," Alberto said. "You do not even have to ask, Enzo. Don't worry. I'll look after her now."

"Thank you, Alberto." Enzo shook his hand. "I knew she'd find a friend in you."

"Alberto's had a busy night," said Clara Finestra. She pulled her head inside the window and turned to face her sister.

"Really?" Rosa asked. She was sitting in an armchair decorated with roses to match her name.

"Oh, yes. The mayor and Miss Bonito."

"The mayor's dead?" Shock rendered Rosa speechless, but only for a moment. Silence did not persist for long in the Finestra household. "Well, I can't hardly be surprised. When one's of a certain size, death does come rather early."

"No." Clara's sharp face lit with delight. She loved knowing things before her younger sister. "The mayor isn't dead. Miss Bonito is. Enzo and his apprentice just carried her up now."

"Let me see." Rosa clawed herself out of the chair and raced toward the window. Pushing Clara aside, she poked her head out into the lane. But she was too late. All of Alberto's living guests had left, and the front of his house was dark.

One by one, Alberto blew out the candles in his workshop.

"There you go," he said, placing the final flame beside the body of Miss Bonito. "That's better. Don't

22

you worry yourself now. I'll look after you. You'll have a proper burial, just like everyone deserves. You can have my coffin." Though she could not see, he pointed to a short, dusty box resting in the corner. "And I'll buy you a plot in the graveyard too. You can have a stone and everything."

To keep the flying fish away, Alberto closed the back window. He turned to leave, but something made him stay. Miss Bonito may have died alone and lain alone for a whole week, but she did not have to lie alone any longer. So, instead of going upstairs, Alberto sat down beside her.

"Good night, Miss Bonito," he said, and in the final pool of light, he laid down his head, closed his eyes and eventually fell asleep.

THE CURIOUS BIRD

That night, while Alberto lay sleeping beside the body of Miss Bonito, a bright little bird flew high overhead. Each beat of its wings made a patch of the stars flicker out, and another made them flicker back on.

The bird was heading out to sea, but it wasn't getting very far. The wind was strong, and the bird's wings were weak. So, instead of flying forward, it kept circling round and round.

"*Twrp!*" the bird cried. "*Twrp!*" it cried again. Its calls echoed across the water, but no calls echoed back.

The bird flapped and wailed for almost an hour before a small light caught its eye. Turning its back on the sea, it soared toward the town of Allora. Houses as bright as its feathers flashed past as it spiraled downward. It flew over cobbled lanes, shingled roofs and glass that glistened white in the night. Then, with a gentle sigh, it landed on a stone windowsill.

The bird shuffled toward two wooden shutters that covered a window. Through a thin gap where both shutters met, it peered into a dim room that flickered with golden light.

A woman's body lay stretched out on a cold table, and an old man, his hair gray, lay sleeping beside her. The bird looked at the woman and tilted its head. A sad cry, formed deep in its chest, echoed across the room. Then it looked at the man. Its inky eyes studied him for several minutes. Finally, as if seeing something it liked, the bird's eyes flickered gold.

"*Twrp!*" the bird chirped. "*Twrp!*" it chirped again.

With a flap of its glistening wings, the bird returned once more to the sky. This time, instead of flying south, toward the sea, it turned north and headed toward the hills that surrounded Allora.

*

"Would you look at that?" said a toothless man sitting in the gutter of Allora's main square. He was talking to a bucket of fish squirming near his feet. "No brighter bird I ever did see."

The man craned back his head and watched the rainbow bird circling by. He'd never seen one like it. Not in the south or in the lands to the north he used to call home.

The man's name was Alessandro Diporto, and as a child he'd heard stories of Allora: stories of how the fish flew out of the sea and fell down, like rain, onto the cobbles below. Then, as a man, he'd had a great idea. An idea as bright as the bird flying high above. An idea that would make him rich.

He left the calm rivers of the north and headed south to make his fortune as the one and only fisherman in all of Allora.

But there had been a fault in his plan. A fault so big, in fact, that it had ruined his plan completely. For what need did a town have for a fisherman when the fish basically caught themselves?

So despite catching 3,089 fish, Alessandro Diporto had failed to sell a single one. This fact had led the townsfolk of Allora to give him a new name. A name that had become so well known everyone had forgotten his old one.

"There he is," people would say as they passed him sitting in the streets with a basket full of flapping fish and a faded sign that read TEN FOR A SINGLE COPPER.

"Keep away from that one," mothers would warn their children as they raced up and down Allora's thin lanes.

"Who's that?" the tourists would ask of the man lying in rags by the gutter.

"Ah," the townsfolk would reply, "he is the foolish fisherman. The one and only in all of Allora."

The foolish fisherman sighed and stared up at the bird in the sky. Yes, he had been foolish to come to this town in search of his fortune. But he knew it would be even more foolish to leave. For what other place in the world could be as magical as this? Where else would he get to spend his nights watching silver fish rain down from the sky and bright birds that were so rare they had never been sighted by a grown man before?

That is why Alessandro Diporto had chosen to stay in the town where everyone called him a fool. He had chosen to stay because when you came to Allora, you just had to tilt your head toward the sky to see magic every day and deep into every night.

WHO WERE YOU, MISS BONITO?

Alberto woke with a start. During the night, cold air had crept through the shutters, and now a piercing chill filled his workshop. He sat up and rubbed his frozen hands together. Slowly, blood and life returned to them. He relit the candle beside him, and a small pool of yellow light warmed the air.

"Good morning, Miss Bonito," he said when her body came into view. "I trust you slept well. We've got a busy day ahead of us." After shaking his legs awake, he opened the shutters, and clean, salty air flew into the room. The hour was early, and a few stars still shone in the sky. His garden smelled of salty dew, and two silver fish lay, as if sleeping, in a flowerpot below.

"Right," Alberto said when he had taken the fish into the kitchen and returned to Miss Bonito. Behind him, the bushes jumped like they had awoken too. "Time to get to work."

Though Alberto had finished his coffin more than thirty years before, it was not ready for Miss Bonito. He had to clean it, sand it, add handles to both sides and engrave her name on top.

"It won't be the best fit," he admitted to Miss Bonito as he began to wipe away the dust. "It will be too wide and far too long. But at least you will fit inside, and I will try to make it comfortable."

While Alberto worked, he spoke to Miss Bonito as if she were still there. In the morning, he told her about his work.

"The trick is in the measurements," he said as a bird tweeted outside the window. "Not too big and definitely not too small. I've never, not in my whole life, made a coffin that was too small."

In the afternoon, he spoke about the weather.

"The sea is wicked today. Wickedly windy too." As if confirming this, the bushes outside rustled loudly and a giant mackerel flew through the window. It landed with a thud inside the empty coffin.

"I don't think I'll be burying you," Alberto said. He pulled the squirming fish out and hurried toward the kitchen with it. "I might have you for dinner."

And in the evening, he talked about the woman herself.

"Who were you, Miss Bonito," he asked, "and why did you come here?"

He could guess where she had come from—she had spoken with a northern accent in life—but he had no idea why she had come to Allora. It was not exactly in the center of things. In fact, it was right on the edge: the final place you went before you could go no farther, the last stop on the railway line before you reached a sea too wild to cross. Had she hoped to start a new life, or did she know her first would soon end?

The sun was setting when it came time for Alberto to place Miss Bonito inside.

"There you go, Miss Bonito." He put a pillow beneath her head. "Nice and comfortable, see?" The setting sun caught the side of her face, and the same golden glow that had lured artists to Allora made her dark hair shine a deep mahogany and her pale skin glow like honeyed milk. If Alberto had not just spent the day building her coffin, he would have mistaken her for being alive.

"Oh, Miss Bonito," he said, as he rearranged her hair over the cushion, "you were far too young to die. It should have been I who went instead."

A FUNERAL AND
A THIEF

Miss Bonito's funeral was one of the smallest funerals Alberto had ever seen. The only funeral smaller was the one he had held for his own family. Even the priest hadn't shown up to that one. He had died of the sickness three weeks before.

In total, five people braved the windswept graveyard at the top of Allora Hill: Enzo the baker, the Finestra sisters, the town's current priest and Alberto himself. The clock tower chimed eleven when they arrived but fell silent when the service began. Unfortunately, two people standing at the back didn't show the same respect.

The Finestra sisters had dressed for the funeral as if it were a wedding. They wore wide straw hats and hideous floral dresses that floated around them in the salty sea air, giving the unfortunate, and unintended, impression that they were as fat as the mayor.

At first, Alberto thought they were making up nasty rumors about Miss Bonito, but when the wind carried their words his way, he heard the mayor's name instead. Apparently, his late-night visit two days before had not gone unnoticed.

"What do you think it means?" Rosa whispered.

"You only visit the coffin maker for one thing," Clara said wisely.

Rosa nodded just as wisely, before asking, "What's that?"

"A coffin, Rosa."

Clara spoke so loudly that the priest paused in the middle of a prayer to see what was wrong. Upon seeing the Finestra sisters, he gave a little sigh, said a silent prayer—*Lord, save me from their wicked tongues*—and carried on.

"He must be dying," Rosa said. "And quickly too. He looked in a rush the other night."

36

"But of what?"

"Tuberculosis? Our cousin had that."

"Or nephritis," Clara mused. "Our other cousin had that. It was awful, wasn't it? Her whole body swelled up—"

"That fits with the mayor," Rosa was quick to observe. "He's been swelling up for forty years."

"And then all that blood," Clara continued. "Remember the mess it made of the carpet?"

"Remember?" Rosa exclaimed. "I was the one who cleaned it up, and it wasn't just blood . . ."

Thankfully, Alberto didn't hear the rest. The wind changed direction and blew their words across the sea. He hated gossip, but at least they were not gossiping about Miss Bonito. Their words were wicked when it came to men, but their tongues were like acid when they spoke of women, particularly the younger ones.

When the service was over and Miss Bonito buried, Alberto headed for home. He had work to do. For the first time in thirty years, he didn't have a coffin of his own, and he felt almost naked without one.

Though Miss Bonito's life had ended, the other lives in Allora carried on. Enzo continued to bake bread every morning, the mayor continued to make laws every day, and the Finestra sisters continued to gossip every evening.

As life continued, deaths did too. Alberto spent the daylight hours working on coffins for those who had just passed away, and when night fell, he worked on his own. Despite the vast number of coffins he made, Alberto never forgot the names of the people he placed inside. Miss Bonito joined this list, unique because he did not know her first name. He tried to think of her often, for he feared no one else would, but as the weeks passed, his mind drifted to other things.

With each coffin Alberto made, he went to another funeral. He had not missed a single one in thirty years. It was when he returned from one of these funerals—*Adamo Totti, maple, 85 × 25 inches*—that he first noticed something was missing.

The first thing that went missing was Alberto's lunch: a sandwich layered with salted ham and cheese. Then, a few nights later, his dinner disappeared: a bowl of stew and two slices of buttered bread. Soon, every time he left the house, he returned to find more food gone.

In the beginning, the thief took what Alberto left on the kitchen table. But soon he or she took things from the cupboards as well: jars of chutney, pickled eggs and two whitefish he had caught floundering on his doorstep.

But while the food in the house was disappearing, something new took its place. Alberto started to feel a change—a *presence*—in the house. He had never been a superstitious man (as a coffin maker, he couldn't afford that), but now as he worked, he could not shake the feeling that eyes were watching him. Not the eyes of the dead, looking up, unseeing. But the eyes of the living, looking everywhere and seeing everything.

Alberto put up with the sneaky eyes and the missing food for three weeks, but when a whole loaf of fresh bread went missing and half a wheel of his favorite cheese, he could stand it no longer. So he came up with a plan to catch the thief.

Alberto set out early for a funeral that did not exist. His plan was simple. He would walk up to the graveyard and then turn straight back. He would be gone for all of ten minutes, long enough to lure the thief out of hiding, but not long enough for them to finish the bowl of steaming porridge in the kitchen.

But as soon as Alberto closed the front door, his plan went awry.

"Coffin Maker! Coffin Maker!" a breathless voice called from farther down the cobbled lane.

Alberto turned to see the sweaty face of the mayor wheezing up the hill.

"Glad—I—caught—you." He came to a stop outside Alberto's front door.

"What can I do for you, Mr. Mayor?" Alberto said, trying to hide his annoyance.

"Could we, er, go inside?" the mayor asked, still struggling to catch his breath.

"I'm actually on my way out."

"Oh." The mayor's face fell. "I just brought those measurements you asked for." With one eye on the Finestra sisters' house, he pulled a piece of folded paper from his pocket and handed it to the coffin maker.

"Oh, good," Alberto said. "I'll be able to order the wood. It might take a while. Golden oak is ve—"

"Shh," the mayor hissed. "I don't want the whole town to hear." Again he glanced toward the sisters' home.

"Of course. Forgive me, please." Alberto slipped the note into his pocket without another word. He said good-bye to the mayor and walked on a little farther. Then he turned back and hurried down the hill. When he reached his front door, he silently pressed the key into the lock and pushed it open.

Alberto stepped into the hall and listened. Sounds came from the kitchen: cutlery clinked, a bottle opened and liquid sloshed into a cup. His eyes lit with triumph and he edged down the hall. But before he could open the door, a person spoke on the other side.

"That was some nice milk, Fia. Real nice."

Alberto paused, one hand on the handle. He did not recognize the speaker, but he could tell it was a child.

"And this porridge," the boy in the kitchen said, delight clear in his voice. "It's still warm. Would you look at all the steam?"

Alberto wondered what to do. He had assumed the thief was an adult. Not for a moment had he thought it might be a child. Should he confront the boy or sneak back outside and leave him be?

Before Alberto could make up his mind, a little bird made the decision for him.

"*Twrp!*" came a chirp from inside the kitchen.

All sounds of slurping, chewing and clinking stopped.

"What is it, Fia?" the boy whispered. He spoke

with a faint northern accent. "Is someone there?"

Alberto pulled back from the door so suddenly that the floor beneath him creaked. Not wanting to frighten the young thief, he edged down the hall. But he was too late. The kitchen door flew open and a boy darted past. A bird—the brightest bird he had ever seen, a bird that swam with shades of gold, turquoise and lapis lazuli—flew in panicked circles around his head.

"Wait," Alberto called. "Come back. I won't hurt you." But the boy and the bird were out the back door before he could catch them.

Alberto stepped into his garden and peered over the fence. The hill was so steep he could see the white froth of the ocean crashing below. He feared the boy would trip and topple down into the raging sea. But, thankfully, his legs remained steady as he bounded through the shrubs with the little bird flapping around his head. Alberto was about to call out again when someone called to him instead.

"Alberto, is that you?" a woman yelled from the garden next door.

"Yes, Clara," he said with a sigh. Farther up the hill, the boy jumped over the gate of the graveyard and landed safely on the other side.

"It isn't Clara," the same voice replied. "It's me, Rosa. Why do you always think I'm Clara?"

Alberto didn't bother replying. He was too busy thinking about the thief. Though he had seen the boy's face for only a moment, it had looked very familiar. That hair. That nose. Those eyes. The likeness of that face he had seen before. He could not be mistaken. It looked like the face of a woman he had buried five weeks before.

A MOTHER'S
BROKEN PROMISE

The boy did not stay in the graveyard for long. As quick as he fled the house at the top of Allora Hill, he fled the town of Allora itself. Keeping to the shadows, he slipped through the town gate and headed north, toward Vita Valley. His legs did not stop until he reached the small cottage that stood in its center.

The boy raced inside and closed the door. Fia—his little bird and only friend—fluttered down the chimney to join him.

"That was close, Fia," the boy said in between gasps for air. "Real close."

45

"*Twrp!*" chirped the bird fluttering beside him. Her wings shone green and then blue and then gold in the dark.

"But at least we got some porridge. And hot porridge at that!"

Fia settled onto the boy's shoulder, and he walked into the next room. In the cold darkness, he picked a faded blanket off the floor and went to sit beside the unlit fire. He wrapped the blanket around himself and Fia and stared at the three pieces of gray wood lying in the fireplace. He had no matches to light the wood, but sometimes, if he closed his eyes extra tight, he could feel heat crackling off imaginary flames.

After the boy's breath returned and his racing heart slowed, a different feeling fell upon him and he sighed.

"I'm still hungry, Fia," he said. "Almost like I haven't eaten anything at all."

The rainbow bird peered out from under the gray blanket and stared into his face.

"*Twrp,*" she said and pointed her beak toward the door.

"But we can't!" the boy replied. "We can't go to Allora. What if we get caught? What if they find out the truth? What if they make me go back?"

46

Fia gave a stern "*twrp*," and gently pecked his cheek. *Well, you've got to find food somehow,* she seemed to say.

The boy looked around the small room. His eyes fell upon an old suitcase and an empty jar that once held strawberry jam. His stomach started to rumble. There was no food here, not even a single crumb on the floor. And even if a fish somehow managed to fly this far inland, he had no fire to cook it. The only food was in the town of Allora.

"This is not how it was meant to be," the boy whispered to the bird beside him. "She said we would be safe. She said we would be okay. She promised that once we got to Allora, we would never go hungry again."

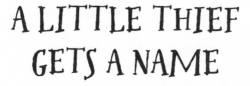

A LITTLE THIEF
GETS A NAME

Miss Bonito had a child," Alberto said to the man lying before him. The man's name was Mr. Adessi, and even in death, he smelled of tobacco. "But how?"

One day had passed since he spotted the boy and his bird stealing porridge from his kitchen, and he was still trying to figure it all out. He had never seen Miss Bonito with a child nor heard mention of one from someone else—not even the Finestra sisters, and they mentioned everything, far more than they should. True, Miss Bonito rarely came into town, but surely after a whole year someone should have seen something. Unless . . . ?

"She was hiding him," Alberto said. "But why?"

Alberto looked down at the silent form that used to move with the life of Mr. Adessi but was now still.

"You never were much of a talker, were you, Carlo? Never mind. I don't think two minds together could solve this mystery. Yet there is a more important mystery to solve, and that is this: who is caring for the boy now?"

By the look of him, Alberto didn't think anyone was. There was no mistaking the thinness of his bones and the sallowness of his skin, a sallowness only a shrinking stomach could bring. Twice Alberto had seen death by starvation, and if this boy did not get more food, he would become the third.

So many questions filled Alberto's mind, but amongst them shone one certainty. The boy was here, he was real, and he needed help.

"So," Alberto said to the stony and silent Mr. Adessi, "that is what I will do. I will help Miss Bonito's son as best I can."

The next day Alberto made breakfast for two instead of one. He ate a bowl of porridge himself and placed another outside in the garden. While he worked on Mr. Adessi's coffin, he snuck glances outside. But the boy and his bird did not return.

Alberto ate the porridge for dinner, and the following day, left out a fresh one. Yet it too went uneaten.

For four days, the food remained untouched, and Alberto feared he had frightened the boy away forever. But then, on the fifth day, the lure became too much, and the boy and his bird returned. Alberto didn't see them come, but he found the empty bowl in the evening.

He wanted to speak to the boy—check that he was okay—but he did not want to frighten him away. After the first sighting, it had taken five days for him to come back. What if he never returned after the second? So, for now, he would leave the food out in the morning, collect the empty bowl in the evening and leave his garden alone in the hours between.

One morning Alberto was getting a plate of food ready to take outside when he heard a knock on the front door. He wondered who needed burying this time. Miss Donati had been looking off-color, and Mr. Grimaldi's cough had gained a worrying tone. But when he opened the door, he found neither.

"Ah, Master Alberto," said the mayor with a jolly rumble. The day was cold, so he wore a thick coat of gray wolf skin. "Glad I caught you. Not too busy, I hope?"

"No, no. I was just making breakfast."

"Breakfast?" The mayor's face grew even brighter. "Why, I might join you." He squeezed his humungous body inside. "What are we having?"

"Sour milk and moldy bread," Alberto lied. In truth, he was going to have smoked cod on three slices of Enzo's freshest bread. But he didn't want to share *that* with the mayor.

"Er, right, well. As it would happen, I've already had my breakfast today. Maybe we could go straight to your workshop?"

"Of course."

When the door to Alberto's workshop was closed and they were inside, safe from prying eyes, the mayor pulled a thick envelope from his pocket and handed it to Alberto.

"What's this?" Alberto asked. He took the envelope and opened it.

"Money. For the coffin."

"But it is too much. Even for golden oak it is too much."

"I put in a little extra . . . for some additions."

"Additions?" Alberto asked.

"Yes. Just a few things." The mayor pulled a scroll from his pocket. It was so long that, when unraveled, it reached all the way to the floor. "Jewels and cherubs and the like. You know, all that sort of thing."

"Cherubs?" Alberto repeated, making sure he had heard right.

"Yes. Those little angels with wings. My mother used to call me her little cherub. I'm going to be buried beside her. Got the plot all sorted. The priest gave me two. It's true. I said, 'No, no. Just the one will do.' But he insisted. Said it would befit one of my position."

The mayor cleared his throat and looked down at his list. "Now," he said importantly, like he was introducing a new law, "addition one . . ."

The talk with the mayor took longer than expected: three hours longer, in fact. A few additions ended up being one hundred and ten. The coffin would still be square and made of golden oak, but the measurements had increased by three inches all around and new fittings had been ordered for the inside and out.

By the time Alberto saw the mayor out, he was

exhausted. Listening to him speak was more tiring than building a coffin. Remembering the food he had left in the kitchen, he hurried down the hall. When he arrived, he discovered someone else was already there.

The little thief Alberto had been feeding for two weeks was now feeding himself a honey sandwich. He must have grown hungry and snuck inside to help himself.

"You eat faster than me, Fia," the boy said in a break between mouthfuls. He took a slurp of milk and tore off another piece of crust. "Here you go." He handed the bread to the bird perched on the bench below. "Don't eat it all at once. It'll get stuck in your throat, and you'll look like a snake that's swallowed an egg."

Though the bird had taken the bread gently, it swallowed it in one gulp and tweeted for more. The boy had just pulled off another bit when he noticed they had company. His eyes darted around the room, searching for a path of escape. The coffin maker blocked the door, but there was a window near the sink.

"Please," Alberto said as the boy raced toward the grimy glass and tried to pull it open. Behind him the little bird flew in panicked circles around the room.

"Please," Alberto pleaded again. "I won't hurt you. Just stay and finish your food. Then you can go out the back way, so no one sees."

The boy gave a final tug before giving up. With his eyes locked on Alberto, he edged over to the sandwich. Forgetting his own warning, he shoveled the food into his mouth even faster and started to choke.

"Be careful!" Alberto raced over to help. "Here." He picked up the glass of milk. "This will wash it down."

The boy took the cup and began to drink. When all the milk was gone, he handed it back to Alberto. With his throat clear, he picked up his sandwich. This time when he took a bite, he chewed it carefully.

"She's a lovely bird," Alberto said of the feathered creature hopping about on the counter, gobbling crumbs as fast as she could. "I've never seen one like her."

The bird was as bright as a peacock but five times smaller. Her right wing was crooked, but her eyes were bright and her beak sharp.

"That's because Fia's special," the boy said.

"I don't doubt it," Alberto agreed with a kind smile. "Fia? Is that her name?"

The boy nodded. He swallowed a piece of his sandwich and said, "She fell out of the sky when she was a baby. She broke her wing. That's why she flies in circles. Her brothers and sisters flew away, even her mother left, but she stayed here with me. I didn't even make her; she wanted to. I think," he said with a shy smile, "she loves me." To stop himself saying more, he took a big bite of his sandwich.

"Well, it's a lovely name for a lovely bird. Do you . . ." Alberto paused for a moment, unsure if he should go on. "Do you have a name too?"

When the boy did not reply, Alberto said, "What a silly question. Of course you do. Are you going to tell me, or will I have to guess?"

The boy remained silent, so Alberto made his first guess.

"You look like a Jacob to me. Yes." He nodded. "Very much like a Jacob."

In reply, the boy took another bite of his sandwich.

"Or how about Pablo?"

Again, silence.

"Bruno?" Alberto asked. He was getting nervous. As soon as the sandwich was finished, he was sure the boy would leave. "Or are you called Antonio?"

At the sudden brightness in Alberto's voice, the boy looked up.

"Antonio?" he said.

"Yes." Hope made Alberto breathless. Had a new Antonio, just like his only son, come back to him?

But the boy looked at him with confusion. That was not his name.

"No," Alberto said sadly. "I did not think so. The silly dreams of an old man. You are a new boy, all himself."

The kitchen fell silent, and Alberto debated his next guess. He decided to take a new approach. "I know! I've got it. I'm sure. Absolutely certain."

Intrigued, the boy stopped eating.

"Emilia," Alberto said. "You are called Emilia."

The beginnings of a smile touched the boy's face.

"Ah, a smile," Alberto said. "Though, I fear, not a name." He frowned for a long moment. The boy watched his face. "I know. How about Teresa?"

The boy's smile grew.

"That must be it," Alberto said triumphantly. "You are called Teresa. I should have known. Would you like some more milk, Teresa?" He reached for the bottle on the bench.

The boy's smile widened and then broke into

a laugh. Startled, like she hadn't expected to hear such a sound coming from the boy, Fia flew off his shoulder and flapped twice around the room.

"I'm not Teresa," the boy said as Fia returned to his shoulder and began to preen her feathers. "That's a girl's name."

"So? Some girls are called Peta, and some boys are called Jess."

"But Teresas are *always* girls."

"Then what should I call you?"

Alberto feared another silence, but instead the boy opened his mouth and said, "Tito. Tito Bonito."

"Tito?" Alberto repeated. "Why, what a fine name." He liked it so much, his chest swelled as if it were his own.

"Do you really mean it?" Tito asked shyly.

"Absolutely. The finest name I've ever heard. Tito Bonito. Tito Bonito," Alberto said again and again. "It rolls right off the tongue. Even an old, tired tongue like mine."

At this compliment, Tito held his head a little higher and a glint of pride shone in his eyes.

"Well, it's very nice to meet you, Tito Bonito. And if you're ever hungry, you may come back here again."

THE COFFIN MAKER'S
APPRENTICE

Tito Bonito came back every day. At first he took his food into the garden and ate with Fia. But as the days grew colder, they began to eat inside with Alberto. The moment they were finished, they would leave—as if they feared something bad would happen if they remained in one place for too long—until one day it started to rain and they decided to stay.

Alberto had work to do, so he left Tito and Fia in the kitchen toasting crusts of bread over the fire. A few minutes later, he heard footsteps near his workshop. He looked up to the sight of

Tito standing in the doorway and Fia fluttering in the hall.

"Don't be frightened," Alberto said. "The dead cannot hurt us; only the living can do that."

Finding truth in Alberto's words, Tito stepped down into the workshop.

"Who's that?" Tito asked, nodding toward the body that lay on a table beside Alberto.

"Miss Alletori. She was a lovely lady. Always took great care in her appearance. She wore the most delicate clothes and bred the ugliest dogs. Awful things, with big, squashed-up faces."

Tito looked down at Miss Alletori. He looked at the brown leather shoes that covered her feet, the light cotton dress that draped her body and the thin necklace that adorned her neck. Then he looked up at the coffin maker and said, "Did ... did my mum come in here too?"

Alberto wanted to lie. He did not want Tito to think of his mother lying in here. But something in the boy's face made Alberto certain he already knew the truth.

"Yes," he said.

The fear that had made Tito's body tense for weeks disappeared. His shoulders drooped, and a deep sadness formed in his eyes. Fia fluttered onto his shoulder and rubbed her head against his cheek. He was so lost in sadness, Tito didn't even notice.

"I know it's hard to lose someone you love," Alberto said, "but try not to think of her in here. Instead, think of her before she came. Think of her when she smiled and laughed and helped you fall asleep at night. It won't take all the sadness away, but it will help you remember happier things."

Tito slowly nodded his head, but the sadness remained in his eyes. Alberto wanted so much to make him happy, but he knew of no words that could magically whisk away grief. It would take time for the boy to heal, just as it had taken time for him.

To help take Tito's mind off his sadness, Alberto picked up a plank of wood and said, "Look here, Tito. Come and have a look at this. This is called spider wood. Can you guess why?"

Tito studied the piece of wood in Alberto's hand. At first he didn't seem to notice anything, but then he focused carefully and spotted something strange. "It looks like it's covered in spiderwebs."

"That's right!" Alberto said. "Now ..." He put

the piece of spider wood down and picked up another. "Can you guess what this is called?"

On that first day in Alberto's workshop, Tito learned the names of five different types of wood. Then he sat by the window and watched the coffin maker work. Alberto took Miss Alletori's measurements, gathered the wood, cut it to size and began to piece it together. A few times the coffin maker went to speak to her, but then Tito would ask a question, so he'd answer the living boy instead.

With each passing day, Tito's chair crept farther across the room, until it was right beside Alberto's workbench. Before Alberto knew it, their conversations turned from the dead to how they would be buried.

"Most are buried in poplar wood," Alberto explained. "It's nothing fancy, but it's easy to work with and doesn't rot."

"Is that what this is?" Tito picked up a scrap of wood lying beneath his feet.

"That's right," Alberto said. "People die without warning, so I have to work quickly. If I work from dawn to dusk, I can make two in one day. The frame is the simplest part—six bits of wood measured, cut and hammered together—but then comes everything else: smoothing the wood, carving it and adding wooden handles."

"Who's this one for?" Tito nodded to the coffin lying before them. Miss Alletori had been buried a week ago, and there was no body in the workshop today.

"For me," Alberto said.

"You?" Tito's face filled with worry. "Are you dying too?"

"I don't think so."

"Then why are you making a coffin?"

"I—I'm not sure. It's just what I do."

"Can I help?"

From that day on, Tito helped Alberto in his workshop every day. Sometimes he was in such a hurry he forgot all about the food waiting for him in the kitchen and went straight there.

Under Alberto's gentle guidance, Tito learned many things: how to smooth the wood, how to cut it, how to join it and how to shape it. He did not work on any of the real coffins. Instead, Alberto gave him scrap wood and a workbench of his own. While they worked, they talked, and for the first time in thirty years, the room echoed with two voices instead of one.

"You know, Tito," Alberto said as the end of another day neared, "I never thought I'd find an apprentice."

"Apprentice?" Tito asked. "What's that?"

"Why, it's someone who is training to do what I can do."

"You mean I can be a coffin maker too?"

"Tito, you can be all sorts of things. Anything you want."

When he heard this, Tito's eyes grew as bright as the candle burning beside him. Alberto imagined he was dreaming of being a doctor, a sailor or a great explorer. But when Tito opened his mouth he said, "I want to be a coffin maker, just like you."

A PARADE OF GOLDEN OAK

The wood for the mayor's coffin arrived early one Monday morning. It was brought by train from the north. It took five days and four nights to chug through the wild mountains that split the country in two. There was so much oak that two extra carriages were added to fit it all in. Alberto was at the station when it arrived, along with ten donkeys who were normally used to pull carts laden with fruit to market.

The donkeys were loaded with wood and led up Allora Hill. The sound of their hooves clobbering against the stony lane and workmen yelling, "Keep

it steady! Keep it steady!" ensured hundreds awoke to the parade. And if anyone slept too deeply, they soon heard about it from the Finestra sisters.

At the first sound of hooves, the sisters threw open the shutters of their house and cast their whole upper selves outside. Though they had been spying over his back fence for forty years, Alberto had never seen their necks so long. They looked like those grand, speckled creatures in books— giraffes—that lived far across the sea.

The wood came on and on. But for a forest, no one had ever seen so much in one place, not even Alberto, who worked with it every day.

"Just take it through to the workshop," he said at least forty times.

When all the wood had been delivered and the train had left the station, Alberto could barely fit inside his workshop. The room was crammed so tightly with wood he had to send Tito in to fetch a tool, darting between the tiny spaces.

For all the crowds that had gathered, one person was not there. The mayor had stayed away while his order was carried into town. Even so, the Finestra sisters pieced it all together. After all, so much wood could only be needed for someone of a certain size. So by midday the whole township of Allora spoke of the mayor and his secret coffin.

The mayor came to check on the wood late in the afternoon. He tapped quietly on the front door and waited for Alberto to answer.

"Well, where is it?" he asked when Alberto led him into his workshop.

"Pardon?" Alberto tried to close the door, but there was so much wood spilling out that it wouldn't shut.

"I said, where is it?"

"Where's what?" Alberto was certain he had heard incorrectly. Surely he was not asking—

"Where's my wood?"

"It's right here." Alberto pointed to the wood covering the floor. "And there." He pointed to the five piles weighing down his workbench. "And out there." He pointed to the wood stacked in the hallway.

"But . . ." The mayor's face drooped as much as his sagging stomach. "It's not gold."

"Well, of course it isn't. No tree is made of gold."

"But it's called *golden* oak."

"It's just a name. It doesn't actually mean anything, not the gold bit anyway."

"But . . ." The mayor looked on the verge of tears. "If it isn't made of gold, why's it so expensive?"

"Because it's as strong as an ox, light as a feather and can float all the way to the shores of Africa."

"But ... but ... it isn't gold," the mayor said weakly.

"Would you like me to order something else?" Alberto asked. "It might not arrive until spring, and you would still have to pay for all of this, bu—"

"No. No." Sense found the mayor, and he shook his little head. "Money doesn't grow on trees."

"It would if they were gold."

The mayor did not appreciate Alberto's joke, but a boy chuckled in the hall.

"What's that?" The mayor's head snapped around, but by the time he looked toward the door, Tito was gone. "Never mind. Must have been my stomach. You don't happen to have any food about, do you?"

"Afraid not," Alberto said. "Though there might be some moldy cheese I use to catch the mice."

"Mice?" The mayor's face paled. They had spread the purple sickness that had killed so many people thirty years earlier. "You have mice?"

"Only in the kitchen," Alberto lied.

And on that note, the mayor decided it was time to leave.

Alberto saw the mayor off and returned to his workshop. He found Tito waiting.

"Did you hear that?" Tito asked. Like a tightrope artist, he was walking along one of the planks of wood. "He thought golden oak was gold. Even I know it isn't gold."

"Well, the mayor isn't like most people," Alberto pointed out.

"Yes," Tito agreed. He jumped off the plank and landed lightly on the dirt floor. "Most people aren't that stupid."

"You rascal of a boy!" Alberto said with a fond shake of his head. "Come now." He waved Tito closer. "Come here and look at this wood."

Quick as a grayhound, Tito was by his side.

"Golden oak is a special wood that must be shaped in a special way." Alberto ran his fingers along the largest section of oak. It would form the base of the mayor's coffin. "Would you like to learn?"

"You mean . . ." Tito's eyes grew wide. "I can help make the mayor's coffin?"

Alberto nodded, and they got straight to work.

A FAINT FLUTTER

Winter came early to Allora, and what a terrible winter it was. Storms built over the sea, and the instant they reached land, the rain turned to snow. The gray cobbles that wound up Allora Hill turned white, and the fish jumped even higher to escape the icy sea. The snow fell so steadily that the tombstones at the top of the hill had a white glaze, like a dusting of sugar on one of Enzo's baked sweets.

Though the days grew shorter, Tito spent longer and longer at the coffin maker's house. He said he was enjoying the work. Though judging by how

71

close he stood to the candles and the fireplace in the kitchen, Alberto had a feeling he was enjoying the warmth even more.

With the mayor's wood ready to be shaped and the yearly influx of winter deaths, Alberto needed all the help he could get. Even Fia was given a task: to fetch tools in her sharp beak. She'd grown so big and strong she could carry whole hammers by herself, and soon, Alberto hoped, she would be able to fetch planks of wood as well.

They were so busy that large blisters appeared on Tito's hands, then cracked and hardened over. Yet despite the thickening of his skin, Tito himself grew softer, calmer and more at home in Alberto's house. Soon he spent more time there than away. But leave he always did, every day one hour before dark. Alberto would watch him race toward the graveyard and vanish, like a shadow, into the approaching night.

Alberto wanted to know where Tito went, but he was too afraid to ask. Though Tito spoke freely about work and Fia, he froze every time Alberto questioned him about anything else. The coffin maker could tell the boy was frightened—he was hiding something—but he had no idea what. And he feared that if he tried to find out, the boy and his bird would disappear from his life altogether.

All was going well until one night a giant storm settled over the town.

"I was down at Enzo's this morning," Alberto said one evening while he and Tito worked on the mayor's coffin. "And he thinks it's going to snow."

"It's been snowing for two weeks," Tito pointed out.

"Ah, but this isn't a little snow. This is a huge storm. Enzo can tell by the fish. Their scales turn gray, and they jump so high they look like tiny pebbles in the sky. There's a saying here in Allora that when it snows the roofs sing. They beat like a thousand drums with the sound of fish pummeling down."

"I thought I saw one fly by the window at lunch," Tito said.

"Ah yes, it was a tuna if I'm not mistaken. You know . . ." Alberto stopped working on the mayor's coffin and looked at Tito. "You can stay here tonight if you'd like."

Straightaway Alberto knew the offer was a mistake. Tito's whole body tensed, and Fia, feathers ruffled, swooped to his side.

"Down here in the workshop," Alberto clarified quickly. "Or in the kitchen by the fire."

"I—I think I better go." Tito put down his hammer and chisel and hurried toward the door. "It's getting dark."

"Of course." Alberto tried to hide his disappointment. It would have been nice to have another life in the house at night. "But can I get you a blanket first? I'm sure there's a spare one upstairs."

Alberto hurried to his room and opened his cupboard. A bright red blanket lay folded at the bottom. It had belonged to little Aida.

"And you haven't had dinner," he said when he handed the blanket over. "Don't worry, I'll fetch you some stew. You can take it with you."

Alberto went into the kitchen and ladled thick fish stew into an empty bowl. When it was filled to the brim, he carefully carried it back to his workshop.

"Here you go, Tito," he said as he stepped into the room. "I've given you a bit extra just in ca—"

Alberto looked around his workshop. Tito and Fia were gone. With a sigh, he walked over to the back window and poked his head outside. A light sleet had begun to fall, and wind swirled his gray hair. In the failing blue light, he caught a glimpse of red near the graveyard on the hill and then Tito and Fia were gone.

"Good night, Tito," Alberto said softly. He closed the window against the chill and went to eat his dinner.

The world was white when Alberto awoke. A fierce storm had swept across Allora during the night depositing a thick, snowy silence. He made his way downstairs in his nightcap. After refueling the dying fire, he placed a pot of tea and another of stew over the flames. While they heated up, he set the table for three.

The tea boiled and the stew bubbled, but Tito and Fia did not appear. Fearing he had locked the back door, Alberto hurried to check. But it opened without need for a key.

Alberto peered outside. Snow covered the world like a blanket. He had to squint against its brightness to see. Everything—the garden, the graveyard, even the sky—was white. Only the sea remained its usual churning blue.

Alberto scanned the snow for Tito, but there was no Tito to see. He feared something was wrong— had Tito fallen down in the snow, or perhaps he was sick?—but then convinced himself that everything was fine. Tito was probably running late. It took a lot longer to walk through snow than grass.

When a full hour had passed, Alberto could wait no longer. A body had been brought in the previous afternoon, and he had yet to get started on the coffin. So, for the rest of the freezing day, he worked alone in his workshop. Every few minutes he glanced toward the door to see if Tito was there, but he never appeared.

"I hope he is okay," he confided to the silent corpse of Mr. Vetrotti.

But, being dead, the old man did not answer.

Fia squawked and soared through the darkening sky. Snow flew into her eyes. She scanned the land below for the town of Allora, but everywhere looked the same. In panicked circles, she flew round and round, searching for a sign of the bright town. Finally, she saw two thin metal lines: the train tracks that led into Allora.

Fia swooped toward the ground and flew along the tracks. She moved in large circles, as her injured wing dragged her down. She flapped and flapped until the tall stone walls of Allora rose before her.

Too weak to rise above the stone, Fia soared through the town gates. Two Carabineers turned to watch the wondrous bird flying through the main square. But Fia did not turn to watch them. She circled past bakeries, taverns, blacksmiths and sweet shops as she searched for the last house on the hill. A few times she fell headfirst into the snow, her wings too weak to carry on. But she always flew back up before the snow had time to settle. And then, as the sky above Allora grew dark and stars began to twinkle above the icy, swirling sea, she saw the house she was searching for.

Alberto was just sitting down to dinner when he heard three loud knocks on the kitchen window. Leaving his stew uneaten, he opened the shutters to find a bird fluttering on the other side.

"Fia?" Alberto said. Snow covered her bright blue head like a hat. "Where's Tito?" He poked his head into the lane, but the boy was not there. "Has something happened?"

"*Twrp*," Fia chirped. To rest her wings, she flopped onto the windowsill.

"What is it? Where is he?"

In answer, Fia rose back into the air and tugged on Alberto's sleeve. *This way*, she seemed to say.

Alberto grabbed the bowl of stew and an unlit lantern and raced toward the door.

Alberto followed Fia down the winding lanes of Allora. The cobbles were as icy as the wind that nipped his cheeks, and he wished he had brought his coat. Lines of light crept out from behind closed shutters, but no one else in Upper Allora was out.

When Alberto reached the market square, he saw two Carabineers standing guard outside the prison. The foolish fisherman lay asleep nearby, huddled under some rags beside a basket full of fish. Keeping close to the shadows, Alberto crept past all three unseen. The last thing he needed was to get caught sneaking out of the town so late in the night. How would he explain himself to the Carabineers? He had a feeling Tito wouldn't be happy if he told them the truth.

Upon reaching the walls of the town, Alberto lit his lantern, and a warm orange light spluttered into life. Above him, little Fia turned right. She flew away from the sea, heading along the train tracks.

Only two trains came to Allora each week: one on Monday morning, the other on Friday evening.

Tonight was a Wednesday, so the line was still. As Alberto followed the tracks, clouds scudded across the sky. Each time the moon appeared, a patch of the world brightened and the wolves in the hills howled. Alberto hoped that none were howling near Tito.

The railmen had kept the train tracks clear, so their progress was swift. But then, a mile out of Allora, Fia left the tracks and flew toward the right. Alberto recognized the direction they headed: they were going to Vita Valley.

Away from the tracks, the snow was thick and fresh. Each time Alberto took a step forward, snow swallowed his legs, and it took all his strength to haul them back out. As the minutes passed, he grew weaker and feared he would have to turn back. Then, despite the thickness of the snow, he felt the ground slope downward.

Vita Valley stood to the north of Allora. A little cottage rose in its center. Built by a farmer one hundred years before, it had lain empty for seven decades before Miss Bonito moved in.

The cottage was small and made of stone. It had a little chimney, a door at the front and four windows spaced evenly around. A thin pile of firewood was stacked against one side. The wood was frozen solid and laced with icicles that shone blue in the fleeting moonlight.

When they reached the cottage, Fia left Alberto's side and flew onto the roof. She hopped along the tiles before disappearing down the cold chimney. Alberto was too old to climb up there and too large to fit down the flume, so he used the front door instead.

At first the door appeared locked, but with one strong budge, it swung open. Snow rolled inside, taking Alberto with it.

Alberto got to his feet and cast his lantern around. The cottage looked more suited to animals than people. Hay covered the dirt floor, and a broken trough rested in the corner. He followed the wall of the room until it met with another door.

The door creaked when Alberto pushed it open, and air as cold as outside washed over him. He stepped into the room and almost tripped over an iron bed. The bed was empty, and he began to fear Tito wasn't there. But then Fia chirped, and he saw a mound of blankets beside the unlit fire.

"Tito?" Alberto hurried forward and dropped to his knees.

Tito's head lay upon a stained pillow. His body was curled up tight beneath Aida's red blanket.

Even in the warm light of his lantern, Alberto could see that his skin was blue.

"Oh no, Tito," Alberto said. He put the bowl of stew on the ground and placed the lantern beside it. Then he raised his hand to Tito's neck. He searched for a pulse, but could not find one.

"I'm too late," Alberto said, sitting back on his legs. Tito must have fallen asleep during the snowstorm and been too cold to awaken. "I should have come this morning. I knew something was wrong. Now the next coffin I make will be for you. I'm so sorry, Tito."

Alberto began to weep, but Fia refused to let him weep for long. She flew down beside him and poked him sharply on the cheek with her beak.

Try again, she seemed to say.

And so, in hope, Alberto raised his old fingers to Tito's thin neck. He searched for a pulse and searched again until finally he felt a faint flutter of life.

"Tito!" he cried. "You're alive!"

THE FLIGHT OF THE LANTERN

Alberto could not carry Tito and his lantern together, but luckily he had help. Using the trick Tito had taught her—the trick of fetching tools from the workshop—Fia carried the lantern in her beak while Alberto carried Tito beside her.

The trip back to Allora took a lot longer than the trip to Vita Valley. By the time they reached the main square, the Carabineers had fallen asleep and Fia was so tired she had taken to sitting on Alberto's shoulder.

Silently, Alberto crossed the square and headed up the hill. The house next to his own was dark, and he breathed a sigh of relief. If the Finestra sisters had seen them arrive back, by first thing tomorrow the whole town would have spoken about the little boy Alberto had carried home in the snow and the bird that had held a bright lantern to guide the way.

Still holding Tito in his arms, Alberto slid the key into the lock and pushed the front door open. He stepped into the hall and headed toward his workshop. He stopped only when he saw his coffin lying inside. Realizing his mistake, he turned around and headed upstairs.

Dust greeted Alberto when he opened the door to his children's old room. Three beds lined one wall, and a boarded fireplace stood in the other. He placed Tito in the bed closest to the door and took the lantern from Fia's beak. She gave a grateful chirp before flopping onto the pillow beside Tito.

Alberto pulled a dusty blanket over Tito's cold body. Then he prized open the old fireplace. A pile of dead leaves and twigs lay inside. Using his lantern, he set the kindling alight and went downstairs to fetch some wood. He built up the fire until it crackled and flared. To keep the warmth in, he closed the door and sat down in a chair beside Tito.

*

Alberto watched over Tito all night. He kept getting more blankets whenever the boy shivered and putting more wood on the fire whenever the flames grew low. It burned so brightly and so fully that by midnight it felt like high summer inside the old room.

Alberto heard the hours pass as the graveyard clock tolled one o'clock—two o'clock—three o'clock—on and on until morning. But the clock on the wall inside never moved, nor did the boy lying beneath it.

That first day, Alberto barely left Tito's side. The blueness faded from his cheeks at midday, but in the afternoon they turned red and his forehead burned with a high fever. It wasn't long before the bird lying beside him started to burn up too. The sickness that burdened Tito had spread to Fia.

Alberto hurried up and down the stairs fetching pails of cold water and placing wet cloths atop Tito's burning head. In his workshop, he would have been terrified if one of the people lying before him had spoken. Yet now with Tito, he wished, hoped, even prayed, that he would speak again.

"I just don't know," Alberto said as day turned to night and he pulled a scorching cloth away from

Tito's head. He also removed a much smaller cloth from Fia's head. "I just don't think I can do it. I've never saved anyone before. I've only buried them." And out of everyone still living in the world today, Alberto wanted to bury Tito Bonito least of all.

The next day Alberto awoke to the sound of two women calling to him from the street.

"Yoo-hoo!" Clara Finestra called as she rapped her knuckles on the front door.

"Only us!" Rosa hollered from beside her.

Alberto moaned and opened his eyes. The last people he wanted to speak to at any time of the day, let alone right after waking, were the Finestra sisters. But he knew he had to answer the door. Otherwise, they'd fetch someone to open it for them.

"Rosa! Clara!" Alberto said with forced cheer when he answered the door. "What are you doing here?" Neither was dead, so they weren't after a coffin. Unless they too were hoping to place an early order.

"We've come to check on you," Clara said.

"We were very worried," Rosa agreed.

"Worried?" Alberto laughed. "Why were you worried about me?"

"Because you missed the funeral."

"What fu— Oh, *that* funeral." Alberto lost his cheerfulness. He had forgotten all about Mr. Vetrotti and his burial yesterday at noon. "Oh, right. I'm just coming down with a . . . a cold." As proof, he offered a little sniffle.

"Ah, we noticed the fire." Clara nodded to the line of smoke trailing out of the bedroom upstairs. "You must be very sick."

"Positively terminal," Rosa agreed. "You haven't lit that fire for thirty years. Would you like us to make you some soup?"

"No. I'm fi—"

"We'll make you some soup," Clara decided. "What neighbors would we be if we didn't make you soup?"

"All right, then," Alberto said with a resigned sigh. It was common knowledge that the Finestra sisters could not cook. They doubled some ingredients, left out others completely and added their own "secret" ingredients that technically weren't even food.

"We'll be back before lunch," the sisters said, and they bustled off to make Alberto some of their infamous fennel soup.

CAKES AND SWEETS
AND STRAWBERRY JAM

Despite taking several sips of Rosa and Clara's soup, Fia got better first. Within days she had recovered from the flight with the lantern and begun to fly in circles around the room. Her beak was a little bent from when she had carried the light, but at least now it matched her wing.

Alberto continued to burn wood at a furious pace, and a constant plume of smoke billowed from the chimney. Every day that passed, the temperature dropped another degree until it was too cold even to snow. Alberto realized that if he had not brought Tito in, he would have died in the same room as his mother.

When he was not forced to work on a coffin, Alberto spent every moment caring for Tito. Despite his doubts, he did not give up on his quest to save the boy. He kept the fire burning constant and bright, kept the blankets warm and sat beside him all through each night. But no matter what Alberto did, Tito Bonito would not wake up. The old coffin maker would have to try something else.

Leaving Fia on guard and one window open so she could fly for help if need be, Alberto went down into town to buy Tito Bonito a treat so sweet it would surely wake him up.

On the first day, Tito went to Enzo's bakery.

"Good morning, Enzo," he called as he stepped into the warm shop. Steam filled the glass cabinets rising before him. Through the milky mist he could see cream buns, doughnuts bursting with blackberry jam and raisin cakes as big as his fist. In the corner, he spotted the foolish fisherman. Enzo must have let him in during the night so he could escape the cold.

"Morning, Alberto," the baker replied with a smile as warm as his shop. He stepped past the sleeping fisherman and approached his friend. "Haven't seen you for a few days."

"Been a bit under the weather."

"Ah, so has my wife. I'll just go and fetch you a fresh loaf."

"Actually," Alberto said as the baker turned around, "I'm not after bread today. I was hoping to buy something sweet."

"So you've finally found your sweet tooth?" Enzo had a little chuckle. "I knew you'd find it one day. How about a little orange cake?"

Alberto looked at the small, round cake Enzo was pointing to and shook his head. He didn't think Tito would like that.

"Do you have anything sweeter?"

"Of course. How about a lemon cream pie?"

Again, Alberto shook his head.

"Sweeter still?" Enzo said.

"The sweetest thing you've got."

Enzo walked behind his glass cabinets, studying each treat in turn. A few times he nodded to himself, but then shook his head. Eventually, he said, "Ah, this is the one. No doubt. You can't get anything sweeter than this," and pulled a treat off the highest shelf. He placed it on a piece of parchment paper and presented it to Alberto.

"What is it?" Alberto asked.

"A triple cream gâteau with extra layers of

custard and butterscotch jam. There's almost half a bag of sugar in that."

"Good," Alberto said. "I'll take it."

On the second day, when Tito had failed to stir for the triple cream gâteau, Alberto returned to Allora's main square and studied the shops rising around him. His eyes soon settled on a pink one in the corner. He walked across the square and entered Madame Claudine's sweet shop.

"Alberto?" old Madame Claudine said when she saw who had just walked through the door. "Why, I haven't seen you in here for thirty years. What was it you bought?" She paused for a moment and stared at the ceiling. "Ah. I remember. A chocolate wolf for Anna Marie, a speckled frog for Antonio and a raspberry fish for little Aida." Her smile turned into a frown. "May those sweet children rest in peace with their dear mother." After making the sign of the gods, she bustled closer. "Now, Alberto, what can I do for you today?"

Alberto took off his frost-laced cap and said, "I'm hoping to buy something sweet."

"Then you've come to the right place. No sweeter shop in all of Allora. Here, let me show you my wares."

Madame Claudine, in her bright, twirling skirts, led Alberto around her shop. She pointed out every sweet that lined the store and told Alberto a little about each one.

"These are the chocolate wolves that Anna Marie loved so much. They're our highest seller, especially in summer when all the tourists come from the north. They don't have wolves up there, you see. The Great Mountains are far too high for them to cross.

"And these ones here"—she pointed to a barrel full of rainbow jelly birds—"are called the Birds of Summer. The color in them will stain your tongue and teeth for two weeks straight.

"And these," she said, stopping before a barrel full of green and brown pinwheels, "are peppermint creams. Nothing wakes you up as swift as one of Madame Claudine's famous peppermint creams."

Alberto was sure the peppermint creams would do the trick. But, alas, they did not. And so, for a third day, Alberto made his way down to Allora's main square. This time he entered the town's only jammery and asked for the owner's finest jar of strawberry jam. He'd heard Tito talk several times about how much he loved strawberry jam.

"Coming right up, Alberto," jam maker Cirillo said. He pulled a large jar off the shelf behind him and wrapped it in red ribbon. As he went to hand it over, Alberto held out three copper coins.

"No, no," the jam maker said. "This jar is for free."

"But I insist." Alberto placed the coins on the counter.

"And I insist even more so," the jam maker said. He picked up the coins and stacked them on the lid of the jam. Then he held both out toward the coffin maker.

"But why?" Alberto said. He could not understand.

"We could only afford spider wood for my mother," the jam maker explained. "But you, Alberto, buried her in poplar. I'd give you every jar of jam in my store for free in thanks for that."

Alberto had been certain that the strawberry jam would wake Tito up. But, alas, just like the triple cream gâteau and the peppermint creams, it failed to make the boy stir.

Alberto began to fear he could do nothing to halt Tito's sickness. He even thought about measuring him for a coffin, but when he had the

94

tape in his hands he couldn't bring himself to do it. Luckily, twelve days after he had carried the boy's frail body home through the snow, Tito Bonito woke up.

"Tito!" Alberto cried. He pulled a steaming bowl away from the boy's pale face. "You're awake!" He could not believe it. He had done it. He had saved Tito Bonito.

Tito looked up at Alberto and then turned to the bowl. He took a deep breath and spoke his first words in twelve days.

"Is that chocolate?" he croaked.

Alberto laughed. "Yes, it is. Chocolate pudding. I made it myself. It was my wife's recipe. It's still warm, and there's cream with it. Would you like some?"

Alberto helped Tito to sit up. When he was propped against the pillows, he spooned some pudding into his mouth. Tito swallowed. Coughed. Spluttered. And swallowed again.

"It's brilliant," he said with a big, chocolaty grin.

When all the pudding was gone, Fia began to peck the bowl clean. In the twelve days Tito had lain still, she had grown bigger and bigger. No longer the size of a sparrow or a magpie, she was now larger than a hawk.

Tito looked around the room. "Where am I?" he asked.

"In my house."

"I've never seen this room before."

"That's because it's upstairs. This was my children's room. But, if you would like, it can be your room now. For as long as you want."

TITO'S FIRST STORY

Tito couldn't believe it. He'd never had his own room before and though his first was filled with things that belonged to other people—dusty books, handmade dolls and wooden horses—he still thought it was the best room in the whole world.

While the winter days grew colder and darker, his new home grew warmer and brighter. After eating lots of chocolate pudding, fish stew and a whole bag of peppermint creams, he grew strong enough to walk and within days was exploring every room in the house. He looked under every bed, opened every cupboard and examined every tool in Alberto's workshop. He only steered clear of one thing: the windows.

Aware that Tito did not want to be seen (though why, he could not be sure), Alberto warned him of two dangers living next door.

"You must be careful," he said one day while Tito was eating breakfast in the kitchen. "Next door live two old sisters named Clara and Rosa, who love to gossip. They tell everyone everything, and if they were to learn that you are here, the whole town would know by lunchtime."

Tito took the warning very seriously. He left his half-eaten porridge on the table and went upstairs to fetch an old sheet. Then he spent the rest of the day tearing it into pieces and placing the cloth over every window.

As Alberto watched each room in the house grow dark, a bad feeling formed in the pit of his stomach. Tito wasn't just worried about being seen. He was absolutely terrified. But why?

Though it only took one extra fireplace to make the whole house warm, Alberto lit them all anyway. Soon, despite all the cloth covering the windows, every room grew bright, and the four chimneys jutting from the roof sent cheerful puffs of smoke into the air, like a signal to another land.

While Tito refused to let Alberto take him down into the town, he did occasionally sneak out into the garden during the day when Rosa and Clara were out shopping or at night when the gossiping sisters were snoring like two freight trains in their beds. Afterward, he would sit beside the fire in his room and Alberto would read him a story.

Before he came to the coffin maker's house, Tito Bonito had never been read a story. So when it came to choosing his first one, he picked it very carefully. He pulled out every book from his bedroom shelf and studied each in turn. He examined the drawings on the front, the drawings inside and the strange words that covered both. Then, finally, he made a decision.

"Can you read me this?" he asked Alberto. He held up a large clothbound book with a drawing of a giant mountain on the front.

"Ah," Alberto said. "*The Story of Isola*. That was Anna Marie's favorite. It's very long," he warned Tito. "It will take many nights to read."

"That's okay." Tito held the book out toward Alberto. "That's why I chose it."

The coffin maker took the book and cleared

his throat. "Right," he said. He put on his reading glasses and, for the first time in thirty years, opened the dusty pages.

There once lived a famous explorer who was born Giovanni Moretti, but went by the name of Gio. When Gio was a child, he would look upon trees no one had ever climbed and climb them. When Gio was a young man, he would look upon raging rivers no one had ever crossed and cross them. And when Gio was no longer young but not yet old, he would look upon mountains no one had ever scaled and scale them. Gio was the greatest explorer the world had ever seen, and his greatest discovery was made at the age of thirty-three.

The mountain Gio decided to climb on the morning of his thirty-third birthday did not look like much from the ground. But once he reached the peak, its true wonders were revealed.

Like fog rising on a winter morning, he saw the mountain for what it truly was. On this mountain the trees weren't made of wood, but silver; the flowers weren't made of petals, but rubies; and the grass, every blade, was made of emeralds. And in amongst these wonders roamed even more: fish that walked on land, horses that cantered through the air and birds that not only flew but swam.

Gio looked down upon all of these wonders and tried to think of a name to call the mountain he had just scaled. But before he could, he heard a whisper on the wind and the whisper said this:

Isola.

"Isola?" Gio said. "Yes. That is a name. That is the name. That is the name I shall call my mountain."

Plucking a ruby flower for proof, Gio returned to the dull world below and began to tell everyone—everywhere—about the wondrous mountain he had found. But even with the proof of a ruby flower, no one believed a word he said.

"It could not be possible," men would scoff when they heard about Gio's latest adventure.

"It could not be real," women would say when told the tale.

"But it is possible!" Gio would cry when he heard them call him a liar. "But it is real!" he would scream to the crowds that gathered to listen. "I swear it is the truth. Here. See. This map." He would throw down a piece of parchment and point to a cross in the middle. "That is it. That is the magical mountain, the magical mountain of Isola."

Most did not believe a single word Gio said.

"The ravings of a madman," they agreed with a nod of their heads.

But some, just a few, looked upon this map and began to wonder if maybe the magic Gio spoke of was not false but real. And so, within a moon of Gio finding Isola Mountain, a small group of men, armed with a map, set out to find it for themselves.

Having reached the end of the story's first chapter, Alberto closed the book and took off his glasses.

"Can you read some more?" Tito asked. He hadn't moved an inch during the story and Fia hadn't either. She'd listened so closely her tail feathers had singed on the fire.

"Not tonight, Tito. I'm feeling quite tired."

"Then tomorrow?"

"All right. I'll read you the next chapter then."

"And the next day?" Tito asked as he helped Alberto return the book to its shelf. "Can you read us another chapter then?"

"I'll read you one every night. On and on until we've read the whole story. Now, Tito Bonito, it's time for all of us to get to bed."

"Alberto's house is looking warm," Clara said as she peered out the window. The sound of a giant mackerel knocking tiles off the roof had pulled her wide awake. Unable to fall back asleep, she'd taken to staring down Allora Lane, searching for the scent of gossip. "Look at all that smoke." Four trails rose out of the coffin maker's house.

Rosa, who had woken to the sight of that same mackerel crashing into her fireplace, hurried over to see. "Why do you think they're all burning?" she whispered.

"Maybe he's cold or—" Clara gasped and her eyes widened with horror. "Oh no," she said.

"What is it?" Rosa asked.

"You don't think . . ."

"Think what?" As usual, Rosa was one thought behind her older sister.

"You don't think he's started to *burn* the bodies, do you?"

Rosa gasped even louder than Clara. Then she poked her head outside and spent the rest of the night trying to catch a glimpse of what the coffin maker was up to.

THE MAN WHO STOLE
THREE APPLES

Tito had been living at Alberto's house for two weeks when they finished the frame for the mayor's coffin and began work on the first cluster of cherubs that would adorn the lid.

"That's very good, Tito," Alberto remarked as he watched the boy carve feathers into a wooden wing. Tito's small hands made the work easy. But it wasn't just that. Tito had a way with the wood that some people were just born with. It was like his heart knew how to shape it and his hands did all the work. Even Alberto's own son, Antonio, had not been able to work wood like that. "I bet you'd make a wonderful blacksmith too. Maybe you could have some lessons with old master Luca down in the forge?"

At the suggestion, Tito's hand slipped and he scraped a deep mark across the cherub's wing.

"Don't worry," Alberto said when he saw Tito's shaking hands. "It was only an idea. You don't have to go anywhere you don't want to."

Tito's hands began to still. He looked up from the coffin and said, "I'd rather just stay here."

"Are you sure?" Alberto asked. "There are many wonderful things out there." He motioned toward the window and the wide world that existed beyond.

Tito shook his head and turned his attention back to the mayor's coffin. He adjusted his grip on the chisel and began to carve another feather into the cherub's scarred wing.

Alberto returned to the cherub he had been carving, but his eyes did not leave Tito. Though he had been looking after the boy for weeks, he still knew hardly anything about him. Tito was like a puzzle he desperately wanted to solve. But how can you solve a puzzle when so many pieces are missing? Hoping to discover one today, Alberto cautiously asked the boy another question.

"Tito," he said, "why don't you want to leave the house? Are you frightened of something? Please," Alberto said when Tito didn't reply. "Please tell me the truth. Maybe I can help."

Tito looked up from the coffin and studied Alberto. Seeing something he liked, he said, "I don't want to leave because then I might be seen."

"By who?" Alberto asked.

"Everyone."

"What's so bad about that?"

Tito paused for a moment, as if he wasn't going to answer. But then he did. "People talk about what they see, and if they talk about me, he might hear. Then he'll come to get me."

"*He*?" Alberto asked. "Who's he?"

"My father."

Alberto gasped. "You never told me you had a father, Tito. I should contact him. Tell him you're safe."

"But you can't!" Tito's eyes widened with a fear so great they doubled in size. "He can never know I'm here."

"But why not? What's so bad about your father?"

Tito's eyes flickered around the room. He looked at the dusty roof. He looked at the empty coffin. He looked at the saws, in five different sizes, hanging from the wall. Then, finally, his eyes returned to Alberto.

"Everything," he said softly. "That's why we ran away."

"From the north?" Alberto asked.

Tito nodded. "We came from the other side of the mountains: just me and my mum. We traveled by train. We would get off at each station and try to live there. But wherever we stopped, he found us. He found us hiding in the town of Trento. He found us sleeping in the stables outside Verona. He even found us hiding in the northern woods, ten miles from the nearest town. Then he'd drag us back home."

"Did he hurt you?" Alberto asked. Worry made the wrinkles on his face grow deeper.

Tito shook his head. "My mum wouldn't let him. She was my protector." When he spoke of his mum, Tito's face lit up like the sun shone upon it, but then a cloud rolled over. "He wouldn't let us leave the house after he found us. But then one night, while he was on patrol, we escaped. This time when we got on the train, we didn't get off until we reached the end of the line. My mum used to call this place magical. She said that whenever anyone got hungry in Allora they just held out a hand and plucked a fish from the sky."

"Tito," Alberto said, "you have been living here for over a year. Perhaps, just maybe, your father has stopped searching."

Tito shook his head. "He'll never stop searching for me."

"How can you be sure?"

For the first time since he came into the coffin maker's house, Tito decided to tell Alberto a story of his own.

One day a man broke into our house and stole three apples. My father is the lead Carabineer in all of Bolzano, so he knew the thief had to be punished. He offered a reward of one gold coin to whoever handed him in first.

It did not take long. The next day a woman came to our house and said the man who had stolen the apples lived on a farm just outside of town.

My father gathered his three best Carabineers and marched out to the farm. He found an old man standing in a small paddock that held one cow, one sheep and one chicken.

The animals were the only three things that the old man owned. He would drink the cow's milk for breakfast, eat the chicken's egg for lunch and, in winter, knit himself a warm sweater made from the sheep's wool.

My father looked down at the old man and said, "Are you the thief who stole three apples?"

Hunger had made the man into a thief, but he was not a liar. So he told my father the truth.

"Yes," he said. "I am the man who stole three apples from you."

"Every thief must be punished," my father said. "You stole three apples, so now you owe me three things."

Winter had only just passed and it was late in the day, so the old man had already drunk the cow's milk, had already eaten the chicken's egg and had already made a sweater from the sheep's wool. But then he had an idea.

"Tomorrow you can have my pail of milk. The next day you can have my chicken's egg. And, when winter next comes, I will knit you a sweater made from wool."

My father thought over the offer and then shook his head. That was not enough. He turned to the first Carabineer and said, "Take his cow."

Then he turned to the second Carabineer and ordered, "Take his sheep."

Then he turned to the third Carabineer and screamed, "Take his chicken!"

"Please," the old man begged as the Carabineers started to drag his animals away. "They're all I have.

Please, just take one. Just take the sheep. Or take two—the sheep and the chicken. Just leave me the cow. Please, you must leave me something."

But my father said, "You stole three apples. Not one."

And then he and the three Carabineers took the animals away.

"You see," Tito said, "that's what my father's like. When something is taken from him, he doesn't stop until he gets it back or he's hurt the person who took it."

"But ... but surely all that about the man and three apples is just a story," Alberto said.

Tito shook his head. "No, it isn't. It's the truth."

The workshop grew so silent that they could hear a lone fish flapping about on the Finestra sisters' roof. Alberto did not know what to say, but Tito did. He had a request. All this talk of his father had made him desperate to see someone else.

"Alberto?" he said. "Could you take me to my mum?"

Now that he knew who Tito was hiding from, Alberto wanted to keep the boy inside forever. But then he looked at Tito's hopeful face and knew he couldn't say no.

"Of course," he said. "I will take you there tonight."

Alberto checked to make sure the lane was clear. Behind him, Tito peered out into the night. It was so late all the lights in lower Allora were out and two rounds of snores filtered through the shutters next door.

"Come on," Alberto whispered to Tito.

Wrapped in a set of Antonio's winter clothes, Tito, for the first time, stepped into Allora Lane. Fia flew beside him, enjoying the late-night air flowing through her wings.

The sound of giant whitecaps crashing into the black water below drowned out the clap of Alberto's and Tito's shoes as they climbed Allora Hill. When they reached the graveyard at the top, Alberto opened the gate. It creaked at the familiar touch of his hand.

"She's over here," Alberto whispered. He led Tito to a small grave near the front gate. "I didn't know her first name or her age, but I did the best I could."

Tito stared at the gray stone for several minutes, his eyes scanning the words engraved on top. "What does it say?" he finally asked Alberto.

HERE LIES
MISS BONITO
WHO DIED ALONE
BUT SHALL LIE ALONE NO LONGER

"But she didn't die alone," Tito said. "I was there with her, all the time."

Alberto's mind traveled back to the night Enzo carried Miss Bonito into his workshop. Enzo's wife had said the sheets of the bed had been warm. Alberto had dismissed her words, but now he realized she spoke the truth. The sheets were warm because of Tito. He must have been lying beside his mother. When Enzo and Santos carried her away, he had followed. That was how he had found himself at Alberto's home.

"Her name was Anita," Tito said. "But her mum called her Ani."

"Her mum?" Alberto's eyes widened. "Do you have other family, Tito? Do you have grandparents?"

Tito shook his head. "They're all dead. My father's the only one left."

To give Tito some privacy, Alberto visited four special graves of his own. His family lay far deeper into the graveyard. Though he attended at least two funerals a week, it had been a long time since he had visited them.

When Alberto reached their plots, he knelt down and spoke to each one in turn.

"Ah, little Aida," he said to the grave that marked the smallest coffin. "I have been giving my scraps to the stray cats every day, just like you asked. And my little Antonio." He turned to the next grave along. "Tito is taking very good care of your things. And Anna Marie, I have been brushing my teeth every night. Well, most nights, and you were right. They have started to look less green."

Alberto cast his eyes upon the final grave. When he read the words on top, his eyes began to water. "Ah, Violetta, my dear Violetta, what can I say to you? We always hoped for another child, and now I have found one. Tito is his name. He's a giant of a little thing. You would have had your hands full with him."

Alberto stayed with his family until the clock tower chimed in a new hour. Then he kissed each stone good-bye and went to fetch Tito.

ALBERTO HEARS
A RUMOR

The rumor started two days after Tito and Alberto returned from the graveyard. Clara was the one Alberto heard it from first. He was cleaning the tools in his workshop one evening when he heard the sisters gossiping over the fence. Usually he ignored them, but when he heard two words in amongst so many—*Bonito* and *child*—he began to listen closely.

"It's true," Clara was saying. Alberto could not see her, though he imagined she was nodding her head with an eagerness only good gossip could bring. "Miss Bonito had a child."

Oh no, Alberto thought. Someone must have seen him and Tito go to the graveyard.

"What type of child?" Rosa asked.

"A little one, like a small person."

"But what *type* of child, Clara?"

"Rather small, I believe."

"No. You misunderstand. Is the child a boy or a girl?"

"Oh. A boy, I believe, called Nito or Beto or Sito or—Tito. That's it!" she exclaimed so loudly Alberto feared Tito would hear. "Tito Bonito."

Both sisters laughed.

"What a silly name," Rosa said.

From where he stood inside his workshop, Alberto's face darkened.

"So where is he?" Rosa inquired when they had stopped laughing. "Where is this Tito Bonito? He didn't die too, did he? Maybe we should ask Alberto."

At the mention of his name, Alberto pulled his head inside. When neither sister called out, he leaned back out into the night.

"No. No. He didn't die. That's the thing. The *mystery* of it all." Clara paused for effect. She paused for so long, in fact, that it lost all effect and Rosa got annoyed.

"Well?" she said impatiently. "What's the mystery?"

"The mystery is that . . . no one knows where he is."

"Then how do you know he even *is*?"

"Because, I believe," Clara said delightedly, "his father has come looking for him. He has come to Allora for the child. *His* child. He has come to take Tito Bonito home."

Alberto Cavello had never been one for gossip, but now he listened closely and learned all sorts of things. Though which things were true and which were false, he could not be sure.

Apparently, or so Clara believed: "Mr. Bonito has been searching for two years. His wife left with the child one night while he was working an—"

"Working?" Rosa interrupted. "Working as what?"

"The lead Carabineer of all Bolzano."

"Ooh," Rosa said. "That's almost as powerful as the mayor."

"He's been following the train line south ever since," Clara said, continuing with her story, "stopping at every station and searching for the son who was stolen from him."

"She must have been crazy to leave a man like that," Rosa added.

"That's what he said. She wasn't right in the head. Kept on making up stories. Saying people were trying to hurt her."

The next night Alberto pressed his ear to the fence even harder than the sisters usually had theirs pressed to his, and he learned of what happened on the night Mr. Bonito arrived in Allora.

"He came asking for a Mrs. Bonito and her son. He went all the way to the mayor, who told him about our Miss Bonito. Said he was right there when they brought her body in. But he assured the man that she didn't have a son."

"Then how did he find out our Miss Bonito was his Mrs. Bonito?" Rosa asked.

"Well, at first he didn't think she was. But then he asked the mayor to describe her and said that was the one."

"But what about his son?"

"Thought he was dead too, but then he went to the cottage and found a pile of blankets and a bowl of stew. He's been living there in secret without her for all these mon—"

"*Twrp!*"

Alberto jumped and spun around. The back door had just opened. Tito poked his head outside. He was holding a large red book under his arm.

Before Tito could speak, Alberto hurried inside and closed the door.

"What were you doing?" Tito asked.

"Oh, nothing," Alberto said lightly. He checked to make sure the door was locked. "Just pruning the flowers."

"Come on." Tito pulled on Alberto's hand. "It's time to read the story."

After all the rumors he'd just heard, Alberto didn't feel like reading a story. But the look on Tito's face made it impossible to say no. So when he had tucked Tito safely into bed and all the shutters were firmly closed, Alberto opened the big red book and continued to tell him and Fia the story of Isola.

When the men armed with Gio's map reached the Mountain of Isola, their faces hardened with anger.

"It was a lie!" they screamed.

"I knew it was impossible!" they yelled.

For the mountain rising before them did not look magical. Not at all. In fact, it looked just like every other mountain: plain and green and positively ordinary.

They were ready to turn back then and there, when one amongst them recalled something Gio the Explorer had said.

"Like a key that must be turned in a lock, we must climb the mountain to see its wonders."

And so, instead of turning back, they continued on. They climbed up the mountain, past trees made of wood, flowers made of petals and grass that was just grass, until finally they reached the peak.

"Would you look at that," the men said, as the true wonders of Isola were revealed.

"He was telling the truth," they all cried at once.

Within seconds of their eyes falling upon the wonders, the men began to grab the treasures for themselves. They filled their pockets with rocks of chocolate, stashed snowflakes made of pearl in jars meant for jam and put droplets of never-ending fire into their dark lanterns. Then they threw ropes into the sky and hauled flying horses to the ground, crammed dancing fish into their hats and pulled swimming birds from the ponds. When they could carry no more, they took the bright wonders of Isola down into the dull world below.

The group of men had intended to keep quiet about the wonders they had discovered. But then one got drunk and told his wife, who told another. And soon word got out. Isola Mountain was real, and for a small price, you could buy one of its wonders for yourself:

A flower of rubies for five gold coins.

A ball of chocolate for three.

And, for ten gold and three silver, you could purchase a lantern full of light that never went out.

But there was one item that was not sold in the streets. Instead, it was auctioned to the highest bidder for the price of three thousand gold coins.

The map that led to Isola was won by a mayor from the north. But, strangely, the mayor had no intention of trekking to Isola Mountain himself. Instead he ordered an army of scribes to make ten thousand copies of the one map he had bought. Then he sent these copies out into the world and sold every single one. Without even setting foot on Isola Mountain, he became the richest man in the world.

But the number of maps did not stop there. For the men and women who had bought maps from the mayor made copies of their own. And soon, within five moons of Gio's thirty-third birthday, every family in the land had seen a map that led to Isola.

TITO LEARNS HIS ABC'S

After the rumors began, Alberto made sure Tito remained inside even more than usual. He did not want the boy to worry, so he kept the sisters' words to himself. For all he knew, Mr. Bonito would leave—give up the search in Allora—before Tito even learned he was there.

But luckily Alberto did not have to worry about keeping Tito occupied. As soon as the rumors started, he began to teach the boy how to read. Alberto had never seen anyone so excited to learn something new. Tito was like a sea sponge that had lain on land for ten years and now, finally, had been thrown into the sea and could soak all the churning knowledge up.

Alberto gave Tito an old ABC book he had used to teach himself how to read fifty years before. On the first day, Tito learned the alphabet all the way to *F*. He was so excited by his progress he did not fall asleep until three o'clock in the morning and was up again at six to learn the letter *G*.

Tito was so busy learning letters he did not have time to listen to any stories, not even the one about Isola. Instead, he spent every night sitting in bed with Fia, who proudly listened as he recited his ABC's.

While Tito practiced his letters, Alberto would go downstairs and work on his coffin. But one night, as he shaped a piece of poplar into a handle, he paused.

Alberto turned the wood over in his hands. He spun it. He touched it. And when his old fingers finally stopped, he didn't see the handle of a coffin anymore but what could, with a little work, be something very different.

A loud squeal woke Alberto at quarter past seven in the morning.

"Look, Fia," Tito exclaimed in the room across

124

the hall. "It's a boat. A real wooden boat. Too little for me, but just the right size for you."

Alberto heard footsteps crossing the hall. A moment later, a shy hand knocked on his bedroom door.

"Alberto?" Tito whispered. "May I come in?"

"Of course." Alberto sat upright to the sight of Tito and Fia charging into his room.

"Look," Tito said, running over to the coffin maker. "Look what I found right at the end of my bed." He held out a little wooden boat that smelled of fresh sawdust. "Did you make it?" he asked.

Alberto nodded sleepily. He had been up all night carving the wood and fitting a piece of cloth to its mast for a sail.

"Is it for me?" Tito sounded afraid, as if it would, in a moment, be taken away.

"Of course it is for you."

"I've never had my own toy before." Tito looked down at the boat and then up at Alberto. "What do I do with it?"

"Why, you play with it."

"And where do I keep it when I'm not playing with it?"

"Anywhere you like."

"And—and—" Tito bounced with another question. "And can it float?" he finally said.

"Why, I don't know. Should we go and see?"

That night when Alberto returned to his workshop he pushed his own coffin aside and made a wooden train with five carriages. The following night, he made a set of miniature birds that fitted one inside the other. Soon he had made so many toys for Tito he had to build a large chest to store them.

While Alberto made toys for Tito at night, during the day the two of them played. They played marbles in the kitchen, blindman's buff in the workshop and hide-and-seek all over the house. Hardly a sound left their lips for fear the sisters next door would hear, but despite the silence, their days became full of fun, and for the first time in thirty years, the house at the top of Allora Hill became a bright and happy home once more.

ALBERTO'S PROMISE

Though Alberto could keep Tito inside most of the time, he could not deny him visits to his mother. So late at night, when the moon was the only other thing up, they would sneak out to the graveyard at the top of the hill.

Tito would go to his mother's grave while Alberto went to his family's four. Sometimes Tito was there for hours, whispering whole days of conversation in one night. Alberto did not know what he spoke about and though, of course curious, never asked. Those words were meant for Tito's mother alone.

One night Tito spoke for so long that the clock tower chimed in a new morning. Alberto, for the first time, had to go over and interrupt. But before they could leave, someone else entered the graveyard.

"Quick, Tito. Hide," Alberto whispered. But he need not have spoken. After one glance at the approaching man, Tito had jumped behind a gravestone and was now hidden from sight.

Alberto watched the man approach. In the dark of night, he couldn't see much. He was tall and dark and, instead of walking, marched.

"Hello," Alberto said when the man drew so near he could ignore him no longer.

The stranger jumped and reached into his pocket. The handle of a pistol appeared. It glistened white in the moonlight.

"Strange time to visit a graveyard," the armed man said.

"And yet," Alberto replied, unable to stop his voice quivering, "both of us are here."

The dark stranger stepped nearer. When Alberto's form grew clear, he loosened his grip on the gun. "Good point. Are you the caretaker?"

"In a way. I'm the coffin maker."

The man's eyes flashed with interest. "Then you

might be able to help. I'm looking for someone. My wife. She's in here somewhere. Bonito's the name."

"Why, you're right here." Alberto pointed to the grave before them. He had suspected the man was Tito's father—they shared a likeness in the shape of their faces—and now he knew for sure.

"So I am," Mr. Bonito said. His eyes skimmed the gravestone and settled on something small and white that stuck out of the winter grass below. "What's that?"

"It's a flower," Alberto said.

Mr. Bonito picked the flower up and snapped the thin stalk in two. Droplets of juice, like dripping blood, seeped out. "A fresh flower that has just been placed."

"Yes." To block the gravestone Tito hid behind, Alberto shifted his body to the left. "I just put it there."

"You?" Mr. Bonito's eyes jumped with surprise and then suspicion. "Why would you—" He took a step forward. His large shadow fell across the old coffin maker. "Leave a flower on *my* wife's grave?"

"Because I knew her," Alberto said with only a slight gulp.

Mr. Bonito's eyebrows rose. "Oh, did you? And in what *way* did you know my wife?"

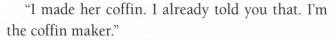

"I made her coffin. I already told you that. I'm the coffin maker."

"Oh." A little of Mr. Bonito's suspicion fell away, but some remained. "Do you place flowers above every coffin you make?"

"Well, of course not. There aren't enough flowers in my garden to do that."

"So why place a flower on my wife's grave?"

"Because no one else does."

"And why would they?" Up until that moment, Mr. Bonito had been quite civil, but now his voice cracked through the air like a whip. "She thought she could take him away from me. But she couldn't. You see, a boy should be with his father. He is mine, and I will have him. That's why she was punished. Death was her curse and so shall it be the curse of anyone who has helped her." Anger made his mouth froth like the sea after a storm.

"Mr. Bonito," Alberto said calmly, "death will be the curse of everyone. Even you."

"Well—" Mr. Bonito's voice grew as icy as the late winter air. "I wouldn't bother leaving any more." He kicked at the flower lying broken on the ground. "She didn't deserve flowers. Besides, I'm sure there's a little hand that's eager to leave another."

"If you're talking about your son, I wouldn't be too sure about that. Miss Bonito lived in this town for over a year, and no one saw this so-called son, not once."

"But I know he was here," Mr. Bonito said. "I found his things, and she never went anywhere without him."

"But perhaps he is here no longer. You have missed a nasty snap in the weather. A chill so deep it almost froze the very sea. I doubt any child living by himself could have survived that."

"Ah, but who said he was living by himself?"

Alberto frowned. "Whatever do you mean? If no one has seen the boy, no one could be helping him."

"No one has *said* they have seen him. They're two very different things."

"Yes, well, it is a possibility," Alberto admitted. It would have been suspicious to deny that.

"A very real one," Mr. Bonito said. He looked across the sea for a moment, as if thinking, and then turned back to Alberto. "You're right," he said. "Someone must be helping him."

"Well, you can't be sure of tha—"

"Yes I can," Mr. Bonito snarled. "There was that bowl of stew. No other bowls in the house looked like that." His eyes lit with triumph. "Here I was waiting for the boy to come back to the cottage. But if he has help, I'll have to do far more than that."

Without another word to Alberto, Mr. Bonito spun on his heel and marched toward the graveyard gate, trampling over graves as he went.

Alberto watched Mr. Bonito leave. When the man was long lost to sight, he leaned over the tombstone behind him and whispered, "Tito, are you still there?"

The young boy slowly stood up. The tombstone was so large, he remained in its shadow.

"Did he see me?" Tito whispered.

"I don't think so."

Tito's body relaxed, but when he spoke, his voice was filled with worry. "What I said isn't false. It's the truth. He really did hurt my mum and do those bad things. I swear it."

Hearing the despair in Tito's voice, Fia poked her head out of his jacket (she was now far too large for his pocket) and nuzzled him gently on the chin.

"I know, Tito," Alberto said. "I believe you."

"Please don't let him take me."

"I'll try, Tito."

"But trying isn't enough. My mum tried every

time, and he caught us every time. You have to promise."

Alberto was not the type of man to make promises he could not keep, but more than that, he was not the type of man who wanted Tito to worry. So, though he feared a day might come when he couldn't keep it, he opened his mouth and said, "I promise, Tito. Now, come around here. There'll be no more hiding behind gravestones for you."

THE SAILING COFFIN
MAKER

N ow that Tito knew his father was back, he had no desire to leave Alberto's house. Even the garden became too dangerous in Tito's eyes. And so, as winter turned to spring, he remained inside, trapped not by a key and lock but by fear: the fear that his father would find him and take him far away.

As the seasons changed, Mr. Bonito remained in Allora. After his conversation with Alberto, he had stopped waiting for Tito to return to his mother's home and now waited for someone to return the boy to him. He had offered a reward of twenty, then fifty, then one hundred golden coins to whoever returned him first. Alberto had never seen so much money—not even the mayor's coffin had cost that much—but he wasn't tempted in the slightest.

Alberto tried his best to keep Tito busy. Their reading lessons continued, and soon Tito could read whole words by himself. Alberto's old ABC book was cast aside in favor of books with proper stories, and it wasn't long before Tito knew all sorts of long, tricky words like *gingerbread*, *bumblebee* and *pomegranate*.

The more Tito read, the more curious he became. No subject was dull to him. Alberto could not enroll him in school, so he tried to bring school to him instead. He taught him all that he knew, not just about wood and coffins, but about history, geography and arithmetic. He even tried to teach him how to cook. Yet no matter how much Alberto told Tito, the boy always had more questions than he could answer.

While Tito could not leave the house, Alberto left every day. In the morning he would walk down the cobbled lanes of Allora, buy a fresh loaf of bread from Enzo and a small bag of sweets from Madame

Claudine and then sit in the main square and wait.

Alberto wasn't waiting to meet someone. Rather, he was waiting to hear someone—anyone—who spoke the Bonito name. By now the reward had climbed to one hundred and fifty golden coins and false sightings of Tito Bonito had risen to at least three each day.

"I saw him climbing the town wall," said a man outside the tavern. "Almost tripped over his own feet. But by the time Mr. Bonito arrived, he had disappeared like a ghost into the air."

"I heard a child crying down by the rocks," said a woman about to enter Madame Claudine's sweet shop. "Weeping for his long-lost father and cursing his evil, crazed mother. But by the time I reached the water, the child was gone, swept clean out to sea."

"It's true. The sea has claimed him," said the foolish fisherman as he awakened from a deep slumber. "I saw it just now, in my dreams. The waves came and took him away, so very far, far away."

Alberto always breathed a sigh of relief when he heard these lies and imaginings. There was no way Tito could climb the walls of the town—they were far too high—and he was not stupid enough to go and sit by the rocks near the sea. But there was one rumor whispered amongst the people of Allora that was actually a truth. And it made Alberto very worried.

"He's started to search the houses," Enzo said one morning as he fetched Alberto a fresh loaf of bread. "Not all of them. But he has searched three already at the bottom of Allora Hill. Apparently someone saw a child's face looking out the window of the first, a child's shoe lying suspiciously outside the door of the second and a whole child—legs, arms, head and all—running in the garden of the third. The mayor says Mr. Bonito can search any home he wants, as long as there has been a sighting. He's even talking about making it a new law."

To keep Tito's mind off his father, Alberto continued to read him stories every night. Or rather, just the one. Tito's favorite: the big red book about Isola.

By now they had heard all about the robbers who had raided Isola Mountain, the crazed queen who had claimed it as her own and the kind farmer who toiled upon its land and bred a whole flock full of diamond sheep. And now, finally, after months of reading, they had reached the final chapter.

Over the space of three and fifty years, men and women, queens and kings, farmers and robbers, all made their mark upon the mountain called Isola. But it was not a good mark. For as the pockets used to smuggle chocolates and pearls turned into buckets and then carriages and carts, the mountain itself began to die. Rubies turned to dust, never-ending fires faded to ash, and snowflakes fell to the ground as ice not pearl.

But the bad marks did not stop there. For, you see, Isola Mountain was far more special than anyone could know. It possessed a wonder that could not be seen or stolen, and that wonder was this: Isola Mountain was alive. Just like you and me, she could think, she could feel, and she could dream. And as she felt person after person trampling over her body and tearing wonders from her skin, she began to cry.

A mountain is a big thing, far bigger than us, so her tears did not form puddles on the ground, but a whole sea across the land. Waves surged up around the mountain as she sobbed, and the people on Isola fled before they drowned. In a single day Isola Mountain became Isola Island.

Isola's tears were as magical as the island itself. She could tame them, control them and move the whole sea at her will. In her anger, she made the water *rage without rest for days, weeks, months, even years. As her land remained untrodden, all of its stolen wonders grew back.*

But just like every living thing, Isola becomes tired and must sleep. While she sleeps her tears still, and if you are fast enough and brave enough, you can sail all the way to her island and tread upon the magical land yourself. And if you are good and true and kind, Isola will let you stay. She will treat you like a mother and fiercely keep everyone else away.

"Wow," Tito said as Alberto closed the final page of the book. "Do you think all that stuff's real?"

"It could be," Alberto replied.

"I'm going to go there one day," Tito said with a stubborn nod of his head. "I'm going to become a sailor and sail all the way to Isola."

"A sailor?" Alberto said. "I thought you wanted to be a coffin maker like me."

"Can't I be both?"

Alberto laughed. "Why, of course you can. You can be the first ever sailing coffin maker. The one and only, sailing from town to town helping to bury the dead."

"And I'll go to Isola first. You can come too," Tito offered.

"That is a kind offer," Alberto said. "But I think I might stay here. I'm far too old for an adventure like that. Though, I'm sure Fia would be very pleased to join you. The way she stares across that wild sea, I think she'd feel right at home out there."

"*Twrp!*" sang Fia, in her most cheerful tone yet.

"Maybe the two of you could bring me back a present. How about a flying horse? Or perhaps a diamond sheep? Or, I know, a flower made of rubies?"

"All right," said Tito. "I'll bring you back two."

THE MAYOR TAKES A
TUMBLE

Tito and Alberto were eating breakfast one morning when they heard a knock on the front door. By now Tito was used to running when death knocked, so he raced upstairs to his room with Fia. Alberto waited for the door above to click closed before opening the one below.

"Ah, Master Alberto," said the man standing on the other side.

"Good morning, Mr. Mayor. What can I do for you?" It had been a long time since his last visit.

"I just came to check on my coffin." He didn't bother keeping his voice down. His coffin was no longer a secret. The Finestra sisters had made sure of that. "Can I come in?"

"Of course." Alberto stepped aside so the mayor could enter. It was a tight fit, and he feared that if the man got any larger, he would need a new coffin. "We're making good progress."

"We?" the mayor asked.

"Yes. You and me." Alberto was quick to correct his mistake. "I think we make a very good team."

"Right you are," the mayor said with a chuckle. "Now, lead the way, Master Alberto. Take me to my glorious coffin."

For once the mayor was pleased with Alberto's progress and, despite the wooden frame, couldn't help admiring his speed and workmanship.

"Particularly those cherubs," he said, pointing to a little cluster near the coffin's base. "What skill you have, Master Alberto."

"Thank you," Alberto said, making a mental note to commend Tito on his work.

"Now, I best be getting on. Wouldn't want to keep you from your work. Though, like I said before, there's no need to rush." The mayor stepped into the hall. "No need at a—"

A loud crash filled the hall, and the whole house

shook as if a ship had plowed through the front door.

"Mayor, are you all right?" Alberto called, racing to his side.

"Yes. Yes. I'm fine." The mayor rocked back and forth like a tortoise stuck on its shell. "Just need a little help getting up."

"Of course. Here, let me." Alberto offered his hand and hauled the great man up.

"Thank you, Master Alberto," he said with an embarrassed chuckle. "Must have tripped over my own fee— Hang on. What's that?"

The mayor hadn't tripped over his feet after all. He had tripped over a little wooden sailboat lying in the hall.

They didn't come until later that night. Tito and Alberto were fast asleep. When they heard the knocks, their eyes flew open and they hurried into the hall. They met in the center, both wearing their nightcaps.

"Who is it?" Tito whispered. Fear robbed his face of all signs of sleep. He had lived with Alberto long enough to know the knock of death. That knock was sad, resigned and, at night, apologetic. This knock was different. It was fast, insistent and angry. Even the mayor did not knock like that.

"I'm not sure." Alberto crept into his room and over to the window. Silently, he opened one of the shutters and peered outside. The sky was dark, but the lane was bright.

"Oh no," Alberto said. Four men were gathered below. The mayor stood at the back, and Mr. Bonito at the front. He could not see the two who stood in between.

"What is it?" Tito rose onto the tips of his toes and tried to peer outside. Alberto closed the shutter before he could see.

"They have come for you," Alberto said.

"What do we do?"

"We must hide you, Tito."

"Just like in our game?"

"Exactly like our game."

"But where?" Tito asked.

Alberto pictured every corner of his house: every fireplace, every cupboard and every bed. But they wouldn't do. Mr. Bonito was sure to check there. He needed someplace else. Someplace no one would even think to check. His eyes lit with an idea.

"Come, Tito. Quickly."

In silence, Alberto, Tito and Fia crept downstairs

146

and into the workshop. Two unfinished coffins lay inside. Alberto couldn't hide Tito inside the mayor's coffin—he would get suspicious if his own was closed—so he led Tito to another.

"Quick, Tito. Get inside, and take Fia with you. Make sure she doesn't chirp. Can you do that?"

With a nod as short and sharp as he was, Tito crawled onto the bench and into the coffin maker's coffin.

"Don't worry," Alberto said as he pulled the lid over the top. A long shadow fell, like a setting sun, over Tito's small body. "I'll come back. I promise."

Alberto closed the lid and nailed his coffin shut.

"Sorry about the wait," Alberto said when he finally opened the door. "I was working on a coffin."

"In your pyjamas?" Mr. Bonito asked.

"Yes, well, I couldn't sleep."

"We heard hammering," one of the men said.

Alberto recognized the voice. He searched the shadowed faces before him. To his surprise, he saw his childhood friend, Enzo. Beside him stood his apprentice, Santos.

"Just closing one up," he said sadly. "So . . ." He turned back to Mr. Bonito. "What can I do for you? Has someone died?"

"Of course not," Mr. Bonito said. "We're here about the toy."

"Oh," Alberto said. "That was nothing. Just a misunderstanding."

"I think you misunderstand *me*, Coffin Maker," Mr. Bonito said. "I have not come here to listen to you speak. I have come here to search your house for my stolen son. Now, step aside or these two men can hold you down while I search."

"Of course." Alberto stepped back so all four men could enter.

"Sorry about this," Enzo whispered as he walked past. "The mayor roped me and Santos in while we were closing the store. Ordered us to come, or he'd lock down the shop forever."

They searched the kitchen first. Everything looked in order, but as they turned to leave, Mr. Bonito spotted two bowls drying beside the basin.

"Hang on," he said, coming to a stop. "I recognize the pattern on those bowls." He picked one up and held it closer. "It is the same as the bowl I found in the cottage."

A triumphant gleam shone in Mr. Bonito's eyes. Alberto feared it was all over, but then his oldest friend spoke.

"Why, I recognize them too," Enzo lied. "I have the same set. Do you, Mr. Mayor?"

"Of course not! They're far too common for me. I get mine ordered in from France."

"*Si, si*. Common indeed," Enzo said. "Why, I wouldn't be surprised if half the town owned bowls like those."

Mr. Bonito growled in frustration. He dropped the bowl into the basin, where it smashed into twenty pieces. Then he turned toward the stairs and climbed up to Alberto's room.

Alberto did not think they would find any sign of Tito in his own room, but then he saw Tito's nightcap lying on the floor. It must have fallen off when he tried to peer out the window. With horror, he realized he was still wearing his own.

"Ah," Enzo said. "I, too, keep a spare nightcap in my room." He picked up the material and placed it in Alberto's hand before the others could notice its small size.

"I think all is in order here," the mayor said with a smart nod. "Shall we move on to the next room?"

Dread slowed Alberto's feet as he followed the four men into Tito's room. Though he'd had time to hide Tito, he hadn't had time to hide any of his things.

149

Tito's room smelled of milk and chocolate. The sheets on his bed were ruffled, toys littered the floor, and ashes filled the fireplace.

"It was cold this last winter past," Enzo said, nodding to the cinders. "We lit every fireplace in the house, even the rooms we kept closed."

"And what about all of these toys and that lantern?" Mr. Bonito snapped. He was starting to suspect the man who had come to help him search was not helping at all. "What excuse is there for a floor full of toys and a bright lantern beside the bed?"

Enzo searched for a lie. When he failed to find one, Mr. Bonito turned to Alberto.

"How do you explain all of this? Is there a special guest staying in this home? A friendly little ghost living in this room?"

"I, er ..." Alberto fumbled for a lie. In his desperation, words tumbled from his mouth. They came so quickly he did not know what they were until he spoke them. "I used to have a son, Mr. Bonito. Just like you. Only I do not have to search for him. For my son died many years ago. I know, for I made his coffin myself."

Mr. Bonito stifled a yawn. He had not come to listen to this old man's story.

150

"Lately," Alberto continued, before Mr. Bonito could interrupt, "your presence in the town and all this talk of your son has opened old wounds, wounds that I have kept bandaged for thirty years. Three decades have I kept this door closed, but lately my thoughts and memories have led me to open it back up. Now, some nights, to my shame, I imagine they are still here with me. Antonio, playing with his toys." Alberto nodded to the wooden train set covering the floor. "Aida, playing with her dolls." He nodded to the dolls in the cupboard that Tito had barely touched. "And Anna Marie, reading her books." He nodded to the open book resting by Tito's bed. It was the one about Isola.

"I blush to admit that I also leave their things lying about the house. So then, when I am tired and walk into a room, I suddenly light up because in my tiredness I forget the past and believe they are still here. My devilish Antonio, my wise Anna Marie and my sweet Aida have just left the room, and if I go upstairs, I will find them lying asleep in their beds."

The room fell silent. Three of the men stood with their heads down, but one, Mr. Bonito, held his up. He kept scanning the room, hoping for a sign, proof, that it was his son living in this room and not the ghost of someone else's. But he could not find one.

"Come on," Mr. Bonito snapped. "We have yet to search the workshop."

Alberto's legs felt like lead as he followed Mr. Bonito, Enzo, Santos and the mayor down the stairs. When they reached the workshop, Mr. Bonito began to search through Alberto's things. He threw aside all of Alberto's tools, kicked away stacks of wood and peered into the mayor's coffin. Then his eyes fell upon the one that had just been nailed shut.

"Master Umberto Romano," Alberto said, nodding to his own coffin. "Poplar wood. Seventy-one by twenty-five inches."

Even though Enzo and Santos had watched Master Romano's coffin—*maple, 76 × 18*—be lowered into the ground two weeks before, neither said a thing. Luckily, the mayor had not bothered to attend that funeral, so he was oblivious to the lie.

"Well, go on." Mr. Bonito nodded toward the coffin. "Open it."

"But . . ." Alberto searched for another lie. He had told more lies tonight than all other nights of his life put together. "But I can't," he finally said.

Mr. Bonito stepped closer to Alberto and reached toward the pocket that held his gun. "Can't or won't?" he said softly.

Alberto gulped and looked to Enzo for help. But the baker looked as lost as he did.

"You see . . ." Alberto said. "I can't open it because—because . . ."

Mr. Bonito was losing what little patience he possessed. He took a step away from Alberto and reached for a hammer so he could open the coffin himself. But just as he was about to prize the first nail free, Alberto thought of something that just might work.

"We can't open it because I'm not entirely sure what killed Master Romano. However, just before I closed the coffin, I noticed a mark. A purple one, behind his ear."

On the other side of the workshop, the mayor's face paled.

"Out," he said, already heading toward the door. "Out!" he screamed as he tripped over a saw that Mr. Bonito had thrown on the floor. "Everyone out!"

"Pull yourself together, Mayor," Mr. Bonito yelled, "and order this man to open this coffin!"

153

"Are you crazy?" the mayor blustered. He hauled himself to his feet and took another step toward the door. "We can't open that. We'll catch what he caught. We'll be dead within days!"

Mr. Bonito looked ready to object. But then the mayor threatened him with an order—"I order you to leave this house immediately or I'll lock you away for three and twenty years"—and he decided it would be best to go. He glanced around the room one final time, his eyes lingering on Alberto and the closed coffin beside him. Then he reluctantly followed the mayor into the hall.

Alberto saw them off from his front door. He waited for all four men to disappear down the lane before returning to his workshop.

"Tito?" he whispered. "It is safe."

He picked up a hammer and began to open the coffin.

THE COFFIN THAT COST
MORE THAN A HOUSE

It may have been safe inside Alberto's house, but outside was more dangerous than ever. When it came to potential gossip, the Finestra sisters were like hawks to mice. They had not missed the bright lights outside Alberto's house, and by the next morning, they had formed a story that soon spread throughout the town.

"They thought the coffin maker had the missing child. It's true," Clara said to Enzo as they bought their daily loaf of bread. "But he didn't. He was just pretending he still had his own."

"Or so he says," Rosa added with a knowing nod.

"Now, I'm sure there's no truth in that," Enzo said as he handed Rosa the oldest, crustiest loaf he could find. "After all, they didn't find him, did they?"

"Just because they didn't find him doesn't mean he isn't there."

"Well, *I* was there," Enzo said, "and every inch of that house was searched, and not a single sign of a boy was found."

Enzo had hoped his words would put an end to all the gossip, but it made the sisters gossip even louder. Not only that, they gossiped about him as well. Apparently, or so Rosa and Clara believed, Enzo was helping Alberto hide the missing boy until Mr. Bonito increased the reward to two hundred golden coins. Then they could hand him over and claim one hundred each.

News of Mr. Bonito's reward had spread, and now tourists didn't come only to see the flying fish but to spot the stolen boy. Rumors swirled, gossip grew, and every day a stream of people walked to the top of Allora Hill. There hadn't been a procession that long since the mayor's golden oak was carried up.

With so many people clamoring outside, Tito did not dare leave the house. Even his late-night

156

trips to the graveyard stopped. He could not go into the garden, either. So enthralled with this gift of gossip living next door and the promise of a bucket full of gold if their rumor proved true, the Finestra sisters no longer pressed their ears to the fence but climbed up and looked over the top. One day Rosa even fell in. Alberto heard the crash all the way from his workshop. Tito did too. He jumped like a startled hare and dived behind the mayor's monstrous coffin.

Now cut off from the outside world completely, Tito threw himself into another world: the magical world of Isola where horses raced through the air and the pebbled shores were made of chocolate. He had reread the story so many times that the pages were fading, and some had even fallen out.

While Tito read each chapter over and over again, Fia would sit on his shoulder watching. For weeks she had refused to leave his side, as if she too could hear the rumors whispered in the town and understood the danger that Tito was now in.

Tito spent so much time reading that he barely found time to help Alberto work on the mayor's coffin. By now most of the cherubs were carved, but they still had to embed jewels into the wood.

So while Tito escaped into the imaginary world of Isola, Alberto pressed ruby after ruby into the wings of butterflies, sapphire after sapphire into the eyes of angels and diamond after diamond into the hair of cherubs. He had encrusted only eight out of eighty motifs when he realized the mayor's coffin was now worth more than his own house.

Tito never complained about being inside, but sometimes Alberto caught him peering through the cloth on the kitchen window as children ran past, playing in the lane. Tito was missing the real world, and Fia, perched restlessly on his shoulder, was missing it too.

TITO LOSES A FRIEND

Death came to Alberto's house, not with a knock this time but a wail, and what a horrible wail it was.

"Master Alberto!" cried a woman in the earliest hour of the morning. "Master Alberto!" she cried again.

With eyes full of sleep, Alberto made his way downstairs and opened the door to Clara Finestra. She was wailing so loudly her breath made a wind that swirled her dressing gown round and round. The moment she saw the coffin maker, she threw herself upon him and said, "Please, Master

Alberto. Please. You must come and help. It's my sister. I think Rosa's dead."

And dead Rosa Finestra most definitely was. Alberto could find no signs of life as she lay alone in her cold bed.

By the time Alberto carried her into his workshop, half the lights in the town were on and little inky heads peered up toward the top of the hill. It was too dark for them to see what was happening, but Clara ensured they all heard.

"My sister," she cried as she followed Alberto into his house. "My sister," she wailed like a banshee. "Oh, my sister," she sobbed. "Dead!" she screamed. "Dead in her bed!"

After sixty-three years of spreading nasty gossip, Miss Rosa Finestra became the subject of gossip herself.

"It was enteritis," a woman told Enzo one morning while she ordered a cake. "It's true. Clara Finestra told me herself. Been sick for weeks, rolling about in her bed. Couldn't even get up to go to the toilet."

"It was a growth deep inside her head," said another. "Had been growing bigger for years and years. That's why she said such silly things. Finally

160

grew so big her brain stopped thinking altogether and she just dropped dead in the street."

But one rumor was spoken far more than any other.

"It was her sister," the townsfolk whispered as her coffin—*rosewood, 65 × 29 inches*—was lowered into the ground. "Clara poisoned her just to get inside the coffin maker's house. She wanted to search for the stolen boy herself and claim the full reward. She always hated sharing things with her little sister."

But despite all the gossip, nobody heard a word from Clara. After Rosa's death, she grew strangely quiet. She hardly ever left the house, and on the rare occasions when she hobbled down into the town alone, she refused to say a thing.

After Rosa's death, Clara Finestra was not the only thing in Allora to fall silent.

"The sea is calming," said Enzo one day when Alberto went to fetch his daily loaf of bread.

"The beast sleeps," Madame Claudine intoned when Alberto bought a bag of chocolate wolves for Tito. "The water's so still even the fish aren't jumping."

This last bit of news sent the townsfolk of Allora

into a panic. No one could remember a time when the waters off Allora had stilled, nor a time when the fish had chosen to swim instead of fly.

"It's not natural," murmured men in the tavern.

"What will we feed our children?" wailed women in the streets.

Only one man in all of Allora seemed happy with this change in the weather.

"A tuna for a silver!" yelled the foolish fisherman as he raced up from the rocky shore. For the first time in eighteen years, he had caught a fish using a line instead of a bucket. And, also for the first time in eighteen years, there were people willing to pay for it.

With no waves crashing below, an eerie silence fell over Allora, pierced only by the foolish fisherman screaming that he had reeled in another fish. Tito was forced to keep quieter than ever, but Fia started to grow loud.

Two days after the water stilled, she sat by the window in Tito's room and screeched—*"Twrp! Twrp! Twrp!"*—over and over again. Tito tried to hush her with food and pats, but she kept on crying out. The next morning when he opened the shutters, she let out a great cry and flew outside.

She soared and dived across the sea for hours, and when she returned she brought them a gift.

"Look, Alberto," Tito whispered as he raced into his workshop. A giant tuna squirmed in his arms.

"Why, you've caught a tunny!" Alberto cried. "I haven't caught one of them in forty years."

"No," Tito said. "I didn't catch it. Fia did."

After that, Fia flew out of Tito's window every morning and returned late in the evening with a new fish squirming in her mouth. She would fly down the stairs, land in a salty puddle on the kitchen table and present Tito and Alberto with their dinner.

With each flight Fia took, her wings grew straighter and stronger. She did not fly in circles so tight, and sometimes Tito swore he saw her flying in a straight line. She flew farther and farther out to sea until one day she went so far that Tito lost sight of her. In the evening, she did not come back.

TITO'S TELESCOPE

Tito sat beside his window and looked out across the calm sea. He had been sitting there for two weeks, waiting for Fia to return. He'd even made a telescope out of paper to help him search. He'd learned about them in one of the books Alberto had used to teach him how to read. But it was no use. Fia was nowhere in sight.

A quiet knock on the door interrupted the silence. Tito turned around, but only for a moment. He knew who it would be: Alberto bringing some type of treat to tempt him downstairs to eat. But it wouldn't work. No matter what it was. He wasn't going to eat a thing until Fia returned.

"Tito?" Alberto called softly from the hall. "May I come in? I've brought you some pudding. It's chocolate. Your favorite."

At the word *chocolate*, Tito's empty stomach rumbled and his mouth began to water. But he wouldn't give in.

"No thanks," he said.

"Please, Tito," Alberto pleaded. "You must eat something."

"No," Tito said. "I'm not ever eating again."

Tito heard the clink of a bowl being placed outside his door and then fading footsteps as the kind and gentle coffin maker walked away. He turned back to the sea and stared at the silent water. No waves crashed against the rocks below. No fish jumped onto the roof above. And no rainbow bird soared and dived and sung as it flew back to him.

Tito wanted to call out to Fia, call out across the sea and beg for her to come back. He knew that if she heard his voice, she would. But he couldn't call out. Not ever. If he did, someone would hear and tell his father. Then he would be dragged all the way back to the north, and he would never see Alberto or Fia again.

*

Alberto climbed the stairs that led to Tito Bonito's room. A bowl of untouched chocolate pudding lay outside the door. He picked it up and replaced it with a new plate.

"Tito?" Alberto tapped on the wooden door. "Tito?" he said again. "I've brought you a slice of Enzo's apple pie."

When Tito didn't respond—he always said something—Alberto grew worried. He opened the door and let himself in. The chair beside the window was empty. All three beds were too.

"Tito?" he said. "Where are you?"

Just like their games of hide-and-seek, Alberto began to search the house. When he had checked every inch of every room, every bush in the garden and every coffin in his workshop, he realized the truth. Tito wasn't hiding. He had run away.

All the lights in Allora were out when Alberto stepped outside. The water below was so calm that even the stars were reflected, like pinpricks of diamond lace. In all his life, Alberto had never seen the sea so still.

Alberto could think of no reason for Tito to go

down into the town, but he could think of a reason for him to go up.

Despite the dark houses below, Allora's graveyard was bright. In the moonlight, Alberto opened the gate and stepped inside. He made his way to Miss Bonito's grave—certain that Tito would be there—but he wasn't.

Panicking, Alberto began to search the graveyard. It wasn't until he looked on the other side of the clock tower that he spotted a small figure standing alone at the peak of Allora Hill.

Alberto weaved through the graves until he reached Tito's side. The boy stood with his telescope pressed to one eye. He didn't even lower it when Alberto began to speak.

"Tito?" he whispered. "What are you doing?"

"Looking."

"For what?"

"For Fia."

"She is too small to see from up here. And it is far too dark. You need the light of a sun, not a moon. Come now, Tito. We must go home before you are seen."

"But what about Fia?" Tito lowered the telescope and looked up at Alberto. A round, red mark covered one eye. "Where is she? She

wouldn't leave me. Not ever. She loves me. Just like my mum."

"Oh, Tito. The sea is a dangerous place. Perhaps— Perhaps . . ." Though they stood in a graveyard, Alberto could not bring himself to speak of death. "Perhaps she is injured and someone is looking after her until she gets better."

"Do you really think so?" For the first time in weeks, Tito's eyes lit with hope instead of despair.

"How about we go home and make her a bowl of porridge? If we place it on the windowsill, she might see it and fly back. Come now, Tito. We must go. It is so late even the wolves are sleeping."

But while the wolves may have gone to bed, someone else remained up. An old woman, missing her sister and thinking of her as she looked out to sea, saw an old man and a little boy standing on the peak of Allora Hill.

For the first time since the death of her sister, Clara Finestra thought of something to say.

A FRIENDLY WARNING

The afternoon felt fresh and bright as Alberto made his way down into town. The air was hot with high summer, and the warmth of the cobbles passed through his shoes and warmed his feet. Today had been a good day, because today was the day he and Tito had finally, after twelve months' work, finished the mayor's coffin.

Despite the events of last night, he and Tito had woken early to complete the piece. Together they had created the greatest coffin Alberto had ever made. Soon he would present it to the mayor, but for now he had something more important to do. He had to go into town and buy his little apprentice a treat.

The bell of the bakery tinkled as Alberto stepped inside.

"Good afternoon, Enzo," he said as he walked toward the counter. He had been into the bakery countless times since the search of his house, but neither had mentioned that night or the lies Enzo had told to help his friend. "Do you have any of those little buns with cream inside?"

Alberto scanned the glass counter. This late in the day, most of the shelves were empty, but there were still a few small treats and a very large pie.

When Enzo didn't reply, Alberto looked up at the baker. His heart skipped a beat. The man looked unwell.

"Are you all right?" he asked.

"*Si, si.* I am fine, Master Alberto. But I fear you are not."

"Whatever do you mean?" Was he the one who looked sick? He did not feel sick on the inside, but perhaps he looked it from the out?

Before he replied, Enzo walked out from behind the counter and flipped the sign on the door from OPEN to CLOSED.

"Clara has seen you and the boy," he said. "She swears on the freshly made grave of her sister. She did not spread it around the town this time. She went straight to the mayor and he to Mr. Bonito."

"But how? When? Wh—" Fear jumbled every question Alberto had, but finally he got one out. "How do you know?"

"Mr. Bonito came in here only just the hour past. He's looking for men to help him search. He said he is going to your house tonight when the bell tolls twelve and you and the boy are sure to be asleep."

Alberto's face whitened with terror, but things only got worse.

"The mayor said he doesn't have to knock this time. He can go straight in. The Carabineers are coming too. Six of them. Before it was just a toy, but now it is a child that has been sighted. There is proof."

"But it's Clara's words," Alberto said. "When did they become proof of anything? I doubt she's spoken a truth in all her life."

"I would have believed you in winter, but this spring just gone has changed her. Since her sister died, she hasn't spread a single rumor. So why now and why this?"

"But—But . . ." Alberto struggled to understand. "Why are you telling me?"

"Because I have known Mr. Bonito for less than a year, and I am certain he is bad. But you, Alberto, I have known a lifetime, and I am certain you are good. If what Clara says is true, then I believe—I am *sure*—there must be a reason you have hidden this boy. You are trying to protect him, from something or someone, though I'm not sure which."

"What should I do?" Alberto said.

"I don't know. This time Mr. Bonito said he will not stop searching until he finds his son. He will tear down your whole house and break apart every coffin. In his anger, I don't dare to disbelieve it."

Alberto searched his crowded mind for a plan. "Can I hide him here?"

"I wish I could help, but you know my wife. She is almost as bad as the Finestra sisters. She knows everything that passes into our house, even a fleck of dirt on my shoe, and makes sure the rest of the town knows it too."

"I understand," Alberto said. "I will think of something. Thank you, Enzo. For all you have done." He turned toward the door, but Enzo called him back.

"It would look suspicious if you left without buying something. Here." He ducked behind the counter and pulled out a large strawberry pie. It was big enough to feed twenty and dusted with granules of golden sugar. "Good luck to you, Alberto," he said as he handed the pie over. "You have been a good friend to me."

"And you to me."

"I will try to delay them as long as possible."

When Alberto stepped outside, Enzo closed the door and flipped the sign back to OPEN.

Alberto returned to a silent house, but it did not remain silent for long.

"Is that strawberry?" Tito asked as he followed Alberto into the kitchen. The smell of freshly baked pie had lured him from the window upstairs.

"It is," Alberto said. He put the pie on the kitchen table and sat in the chair beside it.

Tito stared longingly at the pie, but made no move to eat it. He still hadn't eaten anything, not a crumb, since Fia flew away. To keep his mind off it, he turned to the coffin maker.

"What's wrong?" he asked. Alberto looked sad.

Alberto looked down at Tito's bright face—his cheeks were as rosy as Enzo's strawberry pie—

and then around the kitchen. For the first time in decades, it was bright and clean. He looked at all the life that had returned to his house and to the boy before him, and then he started to cry.

"What's wrong?" Tito said. "Why are you crying?"

"Because they know, Tito. Clara saw us last night. I'm so sorry." His eyes filled with tears, and Tito became a blur.

"Don't worry," Tito said. "I'll hide. Just like last time." And without Alberto's asking, he turned and raced from the room.

Alberto found Tito hiding in the mayor's coffin.

"Out you come, Tito."

"No," the boy replied. He sat up and began to pull the lid over the box. "You have to cover me up. Nail me in, like last time."

"You can't hide in there," Alberto said. "The mayor would grow suspicious if his own coffin was closed."

"Then we'll make another one. If we both work together, it won't take long."

"But it would be too long. They're coming for you tonight."

"Then I'll hide somewhere else. In one of the fireplaces or in a cupboard, just like our game.

I can hide in there all day and night if I have to."

Alberto looked down at the frightened face peering out of the coffin, and his heart broke. "Hiding won't be enough. Not this time, Tito."

"What do you mean?"

"He knows you are here. You have been seen. Now he is sure, and he won't stop until he finds you. Just as he searched every town for your mother, he will search every corner, every fireplace and every coffin in this town and this house for you."

"But why won't he leave me alone?" Tito wailed from inside the coffin.

"Because he thinks that you are his."

"But I'm not. I'm my own person. Just like you said. All myself. And I don't belong to him. I don't want to go with him. I want to stay here with you."

"Even I can't stay here with me, not anymore."

"What do you mean?"

"They know I have hidden a child who is not my own, and I have lied to the mayor. Very few people would look favorably upon that."

"But you didn't do anything wrong. It isn't fair. What will they do to you?"

"Lock me away."

"In prison?"

Alberto nodded. At the prospect, he sank, tired and hopeless, into a chair. Tito climbed out of the mayor's coffin and sat beside him.

"Don't worry," he said. "I know what to do. I'll go back to him. I'll say I was hiding here in secret, all the time, and you didn't know. I was stealing food whenever you went out. They won't be able to get you in trouble then."

"Oh, Tito. How kind. How very generous. But seeing you go back to him would be worse than spending my life in prison."

"It's better than both."

"No, Tito," Alberto said firmly. "You can't go back to him. I promised."

"Then what will we do?"

Alberto thought for so long that the sun fell below the sea and a dark shadow spread over his old house.

"We will run," he finally said.

"Again?" Tito's face fell. "I'm tired of running."

"I'm sorry, Tito," Alberto began, "but it's all I can thi—"

At that moment, a loud crash came from upstairs.

"What's that?" Tito asked.

More thuds sounded in the room above their heads.

"I think it is your father," Alberto whispered. "We have been tricked. He has lied to Enzo to keep us off the scent. He isn't coming tonight. He is coming now. He is already here."

FIA'S GIFT

Though he had just said it wouldn't work, Alberto helped Tito back into the mayor's coffin and closed the lid. He grabbed a plank of wood and headed toward the kitchen.

All was silent as Alberto climbed the stairs, but when he reached the landing, he heard a scraping sound in Tito's room. He tightened his grip, mustered his courage and threw open the door.

Alberto raised his arms in the air, ready to swing, but he didn't. Instead of finding Mr. Bonito on the other side of the door, he saw a very bright and very large bird standing in the center of the room.

Upon hearing the door open, the bird turned to face Alberto. Lumpy, cold porridge dripped from the tip of its bent beak.

"Fia?" Alberto stepped into the room and checked behind the door. No one else was there. Relief made him laugh. The crash they had heard wasn't Mr. Bonito breaking in. It was Fia landing on the windowsill. She had knocked the bowl of porridge over before greedily gobbling it up.

Remembering Tito still hiding downstairs, Alberto raced back to his workshop.

"Tito?" He pulled off the coffin lid, and a little head poked out. "Do not worry. It is not your father. Come and see. Come and see who has flown back to us."

At the mention of flight, Tito jumped out of the mayor's coffin and raced for the door.

"Fia!" he cried when his eyes fell upon the bird standing in his room. "I knew you'd come back. I knew you'd never leave me."

Abandoning the porridge, Fia flew into Tito's arms. She was now so large her wings spanned half the room, and she knocked a bowl of flowers off the mantel.

As Alberto watched Tito hugging Fia, he forgot all about the danger they were in. But then the clock tower tolled seven times and he remembered who else was coming.

Alberto walked over to the window and looked outside. He knew they would have to run, but run where? No trains left Allora tonight, and the Carabineers would surely be guarding the town gate. In despair his eyes dropped from the tower on the hill to the porridge splattered around his feet. It took several moments for him to notice something red lying beneath the largest clump of oats.

Kneeling down, Alberto picked up the clump of porridge and wiped it on his sleeve. When the oats fell away, a little rock of red glistened in the palm of his hand. It was a flower, a flower made from rubies.

Alberto gasped. "It can't be," he said, his voice barely a whisper. Across the room, Tito and Fia were rejoicing too loudly to hear. "It's just a story. It's impossible."

But then Alberto thought of all the impossibilities around him—the flying fish that called Allora home; little Tito, the frightened boy who felt so safe in his house; and the biggest impossibility of all, he, the sad, lonely coffin maker who had found a new reason to live. He began to think that maybe it was possible after all.

"Tito?" he said. "I know where we can go."

Tito stopped playing with Fia and turned to Alberto. "Where?"

"To Isola."

"But that's just a story."

"No, it's not." Alberto held up the ruby flower. "That's where Fia must have gone. She flew all the way to Isola Island and brought us back this flower as proof, so we could go there too."

"But we can't. The sea's too dangerous."

"It has been calm for many weeks, and no trains lead to Isola. Your father would never find us there."

"But how would we get there?"

"The water is calm, so we will take a boat."

"But we don't have a boat. Unless . . ." Tito's own eyes flashed with an idea. "Should we steal one?"

"There isn't a single boat in Allora for us to steal. No one's sailed out into the sea for years." Alberto felt his dream slipping away, but then he had another idea. "Come, Tito. I think we can use something downstairs."

"A coffin?" Tito looked at Alberto like he was going crazy.

"Not just any coffin, Tito. The mayor's coffin. It's

huge. We can both fit in there. Even Fia could too."

Across the room, Fia let out a happy trill.

"But a coffin isn't a boat," Tito pointed out.

"Yes it is," Alberto enthused. "After all, a boat is just a wooden thing that floats."

"But what if Isola Island isn't there?"

"Then we will keep sailing, on and on, until we reach the coast of Africa. And look." He pointed to the jewels encrusting the mayor's coffin. "We can sell all of these when we get there. We'll have enough money to buy a new house. We can start a new life where you won't have to hide."

"Can I go to school?"

"Not just school, Tito. You can go to university."

Tito gasped. "What's that?"

"A place where you learn how to build ships, save lives and draw maps of the world."

Tito liked the sound of university very much, but he still had one concern.

"What will we eat?"

"Why, we'll take Enzo's strawberry pie. That will keep us full for weeks."

Tito and Alberto had to hurry, but they couldn't leave the house yet. The lights of the town were on, and they would surely be sighted. But if Mr. Bonito stuck to his plan, they had until midnight to get ready.

The first thing they did was pack their belongings. Then they packed all of the food in the house: yesterday's bread, half a wheel of cheese and today's strawberry pie. When they were ready, they waited in the kitchen for the lights of Allora to go out. The clock tower chimed twice, and the fire behind them dimmed, but finally, well past ten, they slipped outside.

Keeping to the shadows, for Clara would be on the lookout tonight, they made their way up to the graveyard. They hid their things beneath the clock tower and returned for the mayor's coffin.

With all the jewels encrusting it, the mayor's coffin had grown heavy. Yet Alberto and Tito could still lift it, and they hoped it would still float.

Alberto and Tito hauled the mayor's coffin up the hill. The clock tower chimed eleven as they placed it beside their belongings. Alberto was ready to go right then, but Tito insisted on doing one final thing.

"Please," he said as he pulled on Alberto's hand. "It's important."

So they hurried back to their house and gathered every flower in the garden. Then they

186

sped back up the lane and laid whole bushes of flowers across five graves.

"Enough flowers for a year," Tito said as he arranged the last cluster above his mother's.

"Don't forget this one," Alberto said. He reached into his pocket and pulled out the ruby flower Fia had dropped in the porridge. "This one will last a whole lifetime."

Tito took the flower and gently placed it on his mother's grave. In the moonlight, it twinkled like a lonely ember star.

It was halfway to midnight when Alberto opened the back gate. It let out a pained, piercing creak as its hinges moved for the first time in thirty years. Then, with their belongings stored inside, they carried the mayor's coffin down to the rocky sea.

Warm water lapped at their feet as they moved amongst the rocks. Carefully, they lowered the mayor's coffin into the water. Despite all the additions, it floated with ease. It barely moved when Tito climbed in and only lowered an inch when Alberto joined him.

Alberto looked up at Allora—at the town that had been his home for fifty-five years—for one final time and then pushed off.

The surface of the sea was calm, but the water carried them out quickly. The moon lit their way, and Fia swam through the air as if to guide them. Soon they were so far out that if they turned their heads back to shore, they could see all of Allora branching before them.

The farther out to sea they drifted, the wilder the ocean behind them became. Soon, waves as high as houses crashed into the dark water that led back to Allora. The sea grew so wild that, even if Tito's father and the mayor had pooled all of their money together, they would not have been able to afford a boat large enough or strong enough to follow them. For the first time in his life, Tito was truly free.

Alberto and Tito had been on the water for ten minutes when the clock tower chimed twelve. It echoed on and on across the water, making twelve chimes sound like sixty. The last echo fell silent, and a light appeared at the bottom of the hill. It left the prison gates and marched up Allora Lane. Many more joined it, until a whole chain of flames snaked their way toward Alberto's home.

When the men reached the front door, Alberto's breath caught inside of him. He imagined them smashing the windows and charging inside: their

188

yells and flames and searching eyes. Horror filled him as he realized how close Tito had come to being taken. Before he could imagine any more, Tito spoke.

"Can you see it?" he asked.

"Yes," Alberto replied gravely. "They are at the front door."

"No. Not back there. Out here. Look."

Alberto turned around. Tito held the telescope toward him. The paper was worn and wrinkled, but when he raised it to his eye, he could still see through to the other side. He searched the distant horizon, but could not see a thing. A flicker of doubt formed in the pit of his stomach. Was this all a mistake? Was he taking Tito to a place that didn't exist? But then Fia flew down and pecked the paper a little to the left.

"Yes, Tito," Alberto said, his voice flooded with wonder. "I can see it." Tears glistened in his old eyes. "Truly, I can." Lights—thousands of them, each one as bright as Fia's feathers—clustered together on an island far out to sea. They were invisible from Allora, but the moment you left land, they came into sight, as if you had to be on the sea to see them.

"Here." Alberto put down the telescope and

189

handed Tito a piece of wood. "Take it, Tito, and row. Row as hard as you can."

And so, in the mayor's coffin, the boy, the bird and the coffin maker sailed toward those distant lights and the promise of a new life on the magical island of Isola.

ACKNOWLEDGMENTS:

For Polly, who believed in this story before anyone else did.

For Lucy and Lauren, who took this story and turned it into a book.

And for Anuska, who made this book come to life with her wonderful drawings.

Thank you.